Cocktales

Ca`lab

www.JohnsonPublicationsBooks.com

This book is a work of fiction. Names, characters, places and incidents either are products of the author's imagination or are used fictitiously. Any resemblance to actual events or locales or persons, living or deceased, is entirely coincidental.

ISBN 978-0-98-404168-8
Published by: Johnson Publications
Newtown Square PA
Copyright© 2013 by Ca'lab

Cover Layout/Design by Designs by SheShe
Editors: Carla Dean

Printed in the United States of America

Thank You

I would like to thank my amazing team that worked hard to bring Cocktales to life. I thank my family and friends for all of their continued support.

Prelude

The sound of footsteps echoed off the walls in the hollow space, and heavy breathing could be heard as Sanai's half-parted lips released the air from her lungs. She turned left as she searched the area for her car. Pressing the car remote, she raced with time, hoping to get away clean. She had somewhere to be and could not risk being caught. She knew the outcome would not be pretty.

Sanai ran in four-inch heels with her Macy's bag flopping at her side. Her quick stop at the mall for some last-minute items had just turned into a trip from hell. Thinking quick on her feet, Sanai ducked behind the concrete wall of the parking lot. She held her cell phone up to the sky hoping to be able to get a signal. She needed to be sure it was operating just in case she had to call out an S.O.S.

As she pressed her back close against the wall, she saw a tall, dark man run by scanning the parking lot for her. Once he was at least two hundred feet away, she took off running in the opposite direction, finally making it to her car. Shaken up, Sanai sped off as quickly as possible and headed to her evening engagement. While driving through the streets of the city, she continuously checked her rearview mirror for any signs of being followed.

Hands shaking, Sanai dialed the one person that could understand her. The phone rang twice before someone answered.

"Hey, Sanai. Where are you? I've been waiting thirty minutes for you. I want to be early."

Sanai sighed and attempted to regain her normal breathing. "Girl, I stopped at Macy's to get some stockings for tonight and was spotted by crazy Reggie. And you know a restraining order is only a piece of paper."

"You sure it was him?" Layla yelled. "That's not a good way to start our evening. He never forgave you for loving and leaving him."

Sanai cleared her throat to let Layla know she was not in a joking mood. "The man is sick. He threatened to kill me because I never called him after our first date, and then he stalked me for weeks."

Layla attempted to sound concerned as she changed the station on her car radio. "I remember the story. Well, if you stop giving away the 'goods' with a hat and party favor, you wouldn't have an alliance of stalkers. Now, hurry up. I've been waiting in my car for you to arrive so we can go in together."

Looking down at the phone, Sanai tossed her hair over her shoulder while pulling up to her destination. "Listen, missy, what I do with my *goods* is up to me. I'm here, so come on."

Sanai hung up before Layla had a chance to respond.

Sanai and Layla simultaneously walked through the doors of the downtown convention center. Both were thoroughly dressed for the occasion. The saying "Dress for success" was an understatement when it came to what they wore for the day. Both sported Jones New York women suits; Sanai's suit was cream colored with a white shirt and fishnet satin-seamed stockings that complemented the look, while Layla wore a black suit with the same color shirt underneath the jacket.

After entering, their faces lit up like the sky on the Fourth of July from the sight of the amount of people in attendance. Sanai was the first to speak on how excited they were.

"You see all these people, girl? Everybody in here should leave with a flyer from us letting them know about Platinum Shears."

Walking next to her, Layla replied, "I know, right? It looks like a mini Million Woman March in here."

Her comment regarding the capacity caused them to laugh.

They immediately got down to business and started passing out flyers to everyone present. Once they were done promoting, they made their way to the registration table and stood in the fairly long line. While waiting for their turn, they soaked up all the energy from the crowd. All the women were smiling, shaking hands, and even giving out hugs.

Turning to her right to face Layla, Sanai said, "I'm feeling all this positive energy. It makes me know we're in the right place."

Layla responded with a smile. "I told you that we should come. I just hope we can benefit from being here."

After the brief conversation, they noticed they were about to be next after two other women received their nametags and table arrangements. While ear hustling, Sanai heard the lady behind the registration table congratulate one of the women who was there to receive an award. After the two ladies walked away, Sanai and Layla approached the registration table, where the skinny, dark-skinned lady greeted them with a handshake and a smile.

"Hello, my name is Claudia. Welcome to the 4th Annual Black Women's Professional Networking Party."

Sanai and Layla greeted her, but Sanai was the first to speak.

"Nice to meet you, Claudia. We are here representing for Platinum Shears."

Claudia checked the list for their names.

"Okay, I found your names. Now do you two have your tickets?"

"Yes, we do," Sanai and Layla said in unison, as they went into their pockets, pulled them out, and handed them to Claudia.

"Okay. You're reserved for table seven," she told them, while filling out their nametags.

After handing over the badges to the two women, Claudia told them to enjoy the festivities and then pointed in the direction for them to go in.

Sanai and Layla stepped out of line and put their nametags on the left side of their suit jackets. Then they made their way inside the ballroom. The room was breathtaking, equipped with three chandeliers, a red carpet, and one hundred tables with chairs. The euphoric space filled with women laughing, eating, and sipping on champagne motivated the duo to join in the fun.

They maneuvered through the crowd, saying hello and waving to the patrons while en route to their table. Once they made it to table seven, they found two women already seated there and engaged in conversation. Sanai and Layla smiled and greeted the ladies as they sat down. Sanai recognized them as being the two women who were in front of them in line at the registration table.

"You two were just in line, right?" Sanai asked curiously.

"Yes, we were," Michelle answered.

The ladies then introduced themselves by name and shook hands.

"Now, I couldn't help but overhear that one of you will be receiving the Business Woman of the Year Award," Sanai said, then looked at both of the ladies and waited to see who would respond.

"That would be me," Desereé answered, placing her hand on her chest.

Layla and Sanai expressed congratulations.

"Well, now that we're all here, let's pop these bottles and celebrate," Desereé said as she grabbed one of the bottles of Moët Chandon.

Sanai, Layla, and Michelle grabbed glasses from the center of the table and watched while Desereé popped the first bottle of the night. Desereé poured their glasses first and then Michelle handed her the last glass so she could pour herself some. After the last glass was filled, Desereé raised her glass and gestured for the ladies to join her.

"Let's have a toast, ladies. First and foremost, let's toast for tonight's festivities; second, a toast for the award that's going to be presented to me; and last but not least, wishing success for all of us. Salute!"

After her brief speech, they connected glasses and took their first sip. Even a couple of ladies seated at tables to the left and right of them raised their drinks in respect to the toast. Afterwards, Dereseé was the first to break the short silence between them.

"So what brings you two ladies out for the night?" Dereseé asked before taking another sip of champagne.

Sanai spoke up for her and Layla. "Well, my best friend here," she said, motioning to Layla who was sitting next to her, "decided it would be a great idea for us to come so we can promote our business."

"Oh okay, and what kind of business do you own?" Michelle inquired, joining the conversation.

Both Layla and Sanai pulled out a flyer. Layla handed her flyer to Michelle, and Sanai handed hers to Dereseé. While glancing over the flyers, the two women nodded and then placed them inside their purses.

"So how long have you two been in business?" Dereseé asked.

"It's been a year now," Sanai replied after taking a sip of champagne.

After answering, Sanai became curious to know what Dereseé and Michelle did for a living. However, before she could ask, a loud roar of applause erupted as a tall, light-skinned woman entered the ballroom. She smiled and waved while walking through the crowd like she was the first lady of the Oval

Office. Upon reaching the podium, she spoke into the microphone.

"Hello, ladies, and welcome to the 4th Annual Black Professional Women's Networking Celebration. I'm your host and presenter of the evening, Natalia. Now that the introduction is out of the way, I would like to proceed with our evening. As you know, we have three special ladies receiving awards today, and we have a special performance, as well. So, without further ado, let me present our special guest and CEO of Women Striving For Excellence, Edith Corprie."

The CEO's brief speech was uplifting and celebratory as she encouraged the women to celebrate the life of womanhood boldly. Mrs. Corprie got the crowd going and ushered the special guest to entertain the women for the party segment of the evening.

As melodic sounds oozed from the audio system, the ladies in attendance went wild, while the lyrics of Jamie Foxx's "She Got Her Own" filled the air. During the performance, Layla's phone began to vibrate. She checked to see who was calling; it was her husband. Ignoring the call, she put her cell phone in her purse from where she had pulled it and then went back to enjoying the show. Her phone began vibrating again.

This time, instead of looking at her phone, she leaned over to Sanai, who was mesmerized and singing the lyrics along with the crowd.

"Sanai, Darren keeps calling," Layla whispered.

Sanai sucked her teeth from being distracted. "Girl, you better ignore him."

Layla did just that, but when she didn't answer his calls, he began sending text messages. Layla leaned over to Sanai, and again, she interrupted Sanai from the zone she was in as a result of the singer crooning.

"Now he's texting me," Layla said, almost sounding like she was whining about the situation.

"Look, hand me the phone so I can cut it off," Sanai responded, clearly annoyed.

Sensing something wrong, Dexereé leaned in to see what was going on.

"Is everything okay?" she whispered to the both of them.

"Yes. It's just Miss Newlywed's husband keeps calling," Sanai answered.

Right after she answered Dexereé, the singer completed his last song and the crowd applauded, making it impossible to speak over the noise. Once the hostess thanked the singer, Layla got up and dashed out to call her husband. Sanai just rolled her eyes at the sight of her best friend leaving. Dexereé saw how Sanai reacted and spoke on it.

"Don't worry, girl. Believe me, I've been there before. She's in love. Here, have some more champagne," Dexereé concluded as she poured Sanai another glass.

Sanai accepted the glass and took a sip, but Dexereé could still see Sanai had attitude by the expression written all over her face.

In the twenty minutes that passed, the hostess presented awards to three ladies, including Dexereé. Still, there was no sign of Layla. Sanai sat through the speeches and applauds for each recipient. Finally, after the last one had received their award, Layla returned to the table.

"Sorry, guys. I had to tend to my man," she told them.

"No need to apologize. I totally understand. By the way, congrats on your marriage," Deseree said, while pouring herself another glass of champagne.

Michelle grabbed another one, too, while Sanai just sat back quietly soaking in the rest of the evening.

"Thank you, and congratulations again on your award," Layla replied.

Sanai stood up from her chair and decided to canvass the ballroom to pass out the rest of her flyers. Ten minutes later, she returned to the table, where she observed Layla, Michelle, and Deseree clearly feeling the effects of the champagne as they giggled.

"You ready to go, Layla?" Sanai asked, sounding as if she was still irritated from earlier.

"I'm ready if you are," Layla answered. As she stood up, the thought of getting home to her husband filled her head.

Deseree and Michelle rose from their chairs and extended their hands to thank them for coming. They expressed how much they enjoyed their company.

"Hopefully, we'll get to catch you two at the next event," Deseree said to Sanai and Layla before they departed.

"Yeah, you can expect us there. This was a nice event," Sanai commented.

Layla left them with her own kind words. Then she and Sanai exited the ballroom and out the front doors of the convention center.

*****

3 Weeks Later…

After pulling up to Platinum Shears, Dereseé parked and ran inside. With all eyes on her, she went directly to the receptionist. One would have thought she was on the run from the cops by the frantic way she looked while approaching the young lady. "Excuse me, is Sanai or Layla present?" Dereseé asked, talking fast and with a drawl.

The dark-skinned female frowned up her face. "First, you're going to have to calm down, ma'am. Second, I need to know your name so I can let Sanai know you're here."

Just as Dereseé was about to respond, Sanai emerged from her office.

"Sanai! Thank God you're here. Look, I'm in a rush. My hair dresser had an emergency, and I need to get in a chair ASAP," Dereseé pleaded.

"Don't panic, girl. We got you covered," Sanai told her, then yelled out to Kiki, one of her finest stylists.

Seconds later, Kiki walked up after being summoned.

"Kiki, please give this nice young lady the works," Sanai ordered.

Kiki obliged with a head nod. "Okay. Follow me."

As Kiki proceeded to her station, Dereseé was on her heels.

Forty-five minutes later, Kiki held up a mirror so Dereseé could admire her new hairdo.

"Ooh, I love it, Kiki," Dereseé said as placed the small mirror on top of the station and looked in the larger mirror in front of her, turning her head from side to side so she could view the style from all angles.

Sanai walked over to admire the handiwork of Kiki.

"Great job, Kiki," Sanai commented with a smile.

"You know me, girl. I always do my thing," Kiki replied confidently.

After admiring her hair, Deseree began staring at a flyer that was on top of Kiki's station. Sanai and Kiki stared at her, wondering what she was looking at until she picked it up and inquired about the party.

"Sanai, due to a hectic schedule, I haven't partied in a while. Who's party is this?"

Sanai looked at the flyer and answered, "Oh, that's a party I treat all my employees to every now and then."

"What goes on at these parties?" Deseree inquired, while staring at the picture of a buff, shirtless, light-skinned man who reminded her of a dancer she wanted to kidnap by the name of Inferno.

"Cocktails and male strippers," Sanai replied, then busted a dance move.

Deseree laughed at the quick motion Sanai displayed. She knew by the way Sanai reacted that they must have a great time at the parties.

"Look, I need to loosen up. I haven't had any fun like that since my bachelorette party."

"Well, in that case, I'll put you on the list. You should ask Michelle to come along, too," Sanai proposed, excitement in her tone.

"Cool. I'll give her a call," Dereseé said and then looked down at her watch. "Girl, let me get out of here," she told Sanai, popping up from out of the chair. "I have an important meeting to attend in a few minutes."

She grabbed her belongings while Kiki cleaned off her station. As Sanai began to walk her out, Dereseé stopped and went back to Kiki's station.

"I'm in such a rush that I almost forgot to pay. How much do I owe you, Kiki?" Dereseé asked as she reached into her purse for her wallet.

Sanai walked up behind them and spoke on the situation. "Don't worry about paying. It's on the house."

"Thank you, Sanai. I owe you, girl." Dereseé gave her a hug and then hurriedly walked out of the salon.

*****

Michele and Dereseé entered the private club just as the party was about to start. Women were at the bar purchasing cocktails and conversing, while others were waiting patiently on the sides of the T-shaped stage for the night's entertainment.

Dereseé turned to Michele, who was standing on her right-hand side looking at the controlled chaos. "You want to hit the bar now or wait?"

Michele stood there thinking and took too long to answer. So, Dereseé started humming the *Jeopardy* music as her friend tried to decide on what move to make.

Michele laughed. "Very funny. I was thinking what I wanted to drink, but yeah, let's go to the bar."

They ordered two Apple Martini's and stood at the bar while sipping on them. Dereseé began to scan the room looking for Sanai and the rest of the crew. She spotted them to the left of the bar in an area that appeared to be the VIP section.

"C'mon, girl, let's go over where they're sitting," Dereseé said, tugging at Michele's arm.

They approached the booth where Layla, Kiki, and Sanai were snickering and having a conversation.

"Look who's here," Sanai said, being the first to spot them as they walked up.

Kiki and Layla slid over so they could sit down. Dereseé and Michele sat down and put their drinks on the table.

"So, ladies, are you two ready for the entertainment?" Sanai asked.

"I don't know about this one, but I am," Dereseé answered, while Michele sipped on her martini.

"I like watching naked men. Just never did it in this setting," Michele added after swallowing her drink.

"Do you mind sharing the details?" Sanai asked curiously.

Michele sat there with a confused look on her face, while the others stared at her and waited for her to answer.

"Actually, I do mind," she finally answered.

"Well, rule number one, to sit at this table you have to share details," Sanai told her.

Michele cringed inside at the thought of sharing her sexual secrets. She quickly passed the ball Dereseé.

"Let Dereseé start first. It's the perfect setting to tell about how I saved you from having sex with that stripper at your bachelor party."

Michele's words left everybody flabbergasted. Layla, Kiki, and Sanai all leaned in anticipating the story. Desereé felt a little shy about sharing the story, and to her relief, just as she was about to go into it, the host stepped on stage, saving her.

"Hello, ladies! Are y'all ready for the first entertainer?" the host yelled to the crowd.

"Yes!" the crowd yelled back in unison and began pulling out their money.

"Well, okay. Here he is…the one and only…Inferno!"

Nelly's "Hot in Herre" began blaring through the speakers. A diesel, light-skinned man standing a little over six-feet tall stepped out on stage wearing a vest and Speedos with a stitched on flame design. The women in the crowd began wooing over him and stuffing dollar bills in his crotch as he gyrated his pelvis to the beat in their faces.

Desereé stood up, cocked her head to the side, and blurted out, "Oh my God, it's him!"

She left them sitting at the table laughing at her while she ran up to the stage and began throwing one-dollar bills at Inferno. Overwhelmed with excitement, she pushed two ladies to the side and climbed on stage. Inferno helped by picking her up. The crowd went wild, screams filling the air as they cheered her on.

*****

Sanai and the rest of the clan exited the club laughing and reminiscing about how the night went.

"Oh my God, but did you see how Desereé pushed the two ladies out of the way?" Sanai said while reenacting the scenario.

"Look, Inferno is one sexy mutha. You hear me? Ooh and now I can't wait to get home to my man," Dereseé said.

Layla, Kiki, and Michele said their goodbyes, jumped in their cars, and drove off. Sanai and Dereseé were still standing in the parking lot giggling.

"I really had a nice time, Sanai. We have to do this again," Dereseé told her.

"I propose we do this more often, like monthly. We can all go out for some drinks. You know, like a girls' night out."

"Sounds like plan. Cocktails and fun!" Dereseé said as she hopped in her car.

Before they pulled off, Sanai signaled for Dereseé to roll down her window.

"Oh, one more thing. Next time, I'll be looking forward to hearing your *cocktale* about what happened with you and Inferno," Sanai said.

"Girl, you crazy. Next month…your turn to set up the spot," Dereseé replied as she shook her head and chuckled at the same time.

4 years later...

Eric

Playing with Fire

Eric paced back and forth as he checked his watch for the time. He did not want to be late for any of the festivities on their trip.

"Hurry up," he yelled up to Dereseé.

They only had one hour to get all of their things together and hit the road.

"Come on, Dessie. You know we have to be leaving in fifty-nine minutes."

Dereseé yelled back, "I know. I'm almost done, but you're not even dressed yet."

Just then, Eric heard the front door open. When he peeked his head around the corner from the den, he got a full view of Desereé's backside as she headed out the door.

"Where are you going, Deseree Parker? " Eric asked in a demanding voice.

Turning to look at him, she smiled and gave him the doe eyes. "I'll be right back, I promise. I have to run to the store."

Eric paused, knowing Deseree had been reluctant about going on the trip anyway.

Smiling, he replied, "Fifty-five minutes and counting."

The door closed and Eric continued his frenzy.

The open floor plan in the house allowed for plenty of light and space for the power couple to move around. The bright colored artwork and nine-foot ceilings made for a spectacular atmosphere. Eric hurried around trying to get his last-minute items in his bag for his impromptu get away with his wife. He could not wait to partake in all of the adult festivities that were planned. From the things listed on the itinerary, the group giving the getaway was very adventurous. With the trip starting on a Wednesday and ending on Saturday night, this gave Eric a sense that the trip would be anything but traditional.

Eric walked to the kitchen while adjusting his Rolex. He smiled at the memory of his father passing it to him when he graduated law school. His Rolex was old, but just like old money, it got better with time. The Rolex also brought him plenty of luck in his life and career.

Thirsty from all the running around he had done, Eric grabbed a glass from the cabinet above the counter and bent down in the fridge to get the orange juice from the bottom shelf.

He heard the door slam and was happy Dereseé only took about fifteen minutes to run her errand. Standing upright, Eric prepared to tease her.

"What did you forg—"

He stopped in mid-sentence, and the glass crashed to the floor. There stood the object of his desire and worst nightmare, half naked.

Approaching the woman, he said, "What are you doing here? How did you get in?"

The woman pulled him close to her and replied, "Oh, you're not happy to see me? You know the rich folk never lock their doors."

As Eric stood with his mouth hanging open, she grabbed his crotch. Eric's manhood responded quickly even though he was scared shitless. Despite being shocked, he attempted to gain control of the situation.

"Come on, sweetie. You know this is dangerous. Dessie will be back any moment. You have to leave now."

Eric walked away as he tried to adjust his erection, but the woman did not move. In fact, she just silently stood there while perusing Eric's tall chocolate body from head to toe. She moved in closer to him and broke the silence.

With half-parted lips next to his ear, she whispered, "You know what I came for, and by the looks of it, I will be getting it quick and easy. You're already in your drawers."

Eric pushed away even though he wanted to consume every inch of her slowly so he could savor the experience. "You've lost your mind. In my home where my wife and I stay? No way."

She pulled him close to her and kissed his juicy lips, causing him to let out a masculine moan. She then slid down to the floor and kissed around his pelvis. Eric's eyes closed and his head fell back. She placed her soft, wet mouth on his manhood through the slit in his boxers. His erection intensified.

"See, I know what you need, daddy. Let me take care of you."

The sound of her voice snapped him out of his trance. Eric opened his eyes and reached down, grabbing her hair with force.

"Look, you know I want you, but I can't. I have to leave on a trip with my wife in a few minutes. If she found us here, she would kill us both."

The seductress became undone. "A trip!" she yelled. "You wouldn't even be going on this trip if it wasn't for me! You would still be sexually unfulfilled with your wife. Remember, I'm the only one who can make you feel like I do. You still belong to me."

Eric attempted to calm her down, while praying Deseree didn't find the pair half naked in their kitchen. Seconds later, Eric heard Deseree's car pulling into the driveway.

"Oh shit! She will not find us here like this. Hide or die!" Eric said, then shoved her under the storage area in the kitchen island. "If you value your life, you will be absolutely quiet," he added.

Deseree entered the house to find Eric in the kitchen half-dressed and cleaning up the broken glass.

"What happened, Eric? Are you okay?" a concerned Deseree asked.

Eric held out his hand, urging her to stay back. "I'm fine, Dessie. I just dropped my juice rushing. Go start gathering your bags. I'll be done in a minute and will meet you upstairs. We have about ten minutes left."

Doing as told, Dereseé turned and headed to the bedroom.

Eric

Fantasy Island

Eric and Dereeé arrived at the hotel just in time. He pulled up to the entrance and proceeded to get the bags out of the trunk. The outside was beautiful. Gold-trimmed double doors swung open as Dereeé took a deep breath while watching the valet driver cruise away in their Benz. Eric was excited to be there and couldn't hide it. He had done a lot of coaxing and suggesting that they put some spice in their love life. Just as she was when he first mentioned it, Dereeé was still reluctant, but she went along for the experience to please her man.

The bellhop hurried their luggage to their spacious suite. Eric rushed Dereeé in the room, urging her to hurry up and change for the evening. They were headed to the swingers' ball and both were virgins to this new lifestyle. One of the reasons being that Dereeé liked her sex like a duet—two people only.

Dereseé placed her luggage in the corner of the room and proceeded to disrobe. Eric stood in the background excited like he was the first time he saw her naked body. Dereseé's perky breasts, which were the color of warm butter, entranced him. Her caramel colored nipples became erect upon being exposed to the air. Dereseé caught Eric staring at her and put on a show for her audience, prancing around and causing her round booty to sway from side to side.

I know my body still excites him. I can feel it, she thought as she disappeared into the bathroom, closing the door behind her as if playing a game of cat and mouse.

Eric stood in front of his luggage selecting his duds for the evening. He couldn't wait to get in the mix of all the action. For the past three months, Eric had grown a newfound appreciation for sex and was willing to take his pleasure to another level. Thinking back to when his libido increased made him yearn to contact his muse and make things right. So, he sent her a text message in an attempt to apologize for their earlier encounter.

Wanting to experience pure pleasure was his mission; bringing his wife along with him to share in the experience was icing on the cake. He felt a tingling in his groin as his manhood rose from the thought of Dereseé's beautiful body touching another woman's skin. He would have to come up with a plan to make his fantasy actually come true.

To relieve his sexual tension, Eric disrobed and joined Dereseé in the shower. He figured a little one-on-one action would be the appetizer before the main course later in the evening. Eric approached the shower in full glory. The sound of the water hitting her naked body gave him chills.

Eric approached Dereseé from behind like a lion casing their prey. With a bit of aggression, he bit and licked her neck. Dereseé moaned and jerked each time his soft lips met her skin. His chocolate skin against her soft, caramel skin made for a beautiful picture.

"Put your hands on the wall and spread those sexy legs, baby," Eric whispered.

Dereseé followed orders without hesitating. Eric started to grind against her plump bottom while running his hands up her wet arms. Dereseé arched her back, anticipating Eric entering her cave. He continued to rub his rod against her, rimming her entrance. She let out loud moans as she shivered from the pleasurable sensation.

"This feels sooo good, baby. Keep going."

Eric continued to tease her as he reached up and grabbed the showerhead, removing it from its holder. Eric pointed the pulsating device at Dereseé's crotch. The strong flow of water massaged her clitoris, sending her into multiple orgasms.

"Ahhhh, Eric, I'm cummmmmin'!" Dereseé screamed.

While pressing his rod against her rear, Eric held the showerhead steady with his one hand and pulled on her nipple with his other.

"Oooooooo, shit! I can't wait no more. Stick it in now. I'm coming again. Eric, please!" she moaned.

Eric dropped the showerhead and slid his love stick deep inside Dereseé as she squirted like a water hose. He massaged her insides until he couldn't take it any longer.

"Dessie, I love this!" he proclaimed.

Two pumps later, they both yelled in unison as they reached the peak of ecstasy. They fell to the shower floor out of breath as the showerhead continued to spray water throughout the bathroom. No doubt, their adventure was off to a great start.\

Desereé

In Too Deep

The light from the half cracked curtains found a home on Desereé's right cheek. She awoke to the sun's rays warming her face. Desereé attempted to lift her head from the pillow and open her heavy eyes with no success.

Holding her forehead, she whispered, "How did I get this brain-crushing headache?"

Desereé` tried to make sense of the night before; she didn't know what was real and what was all in her dreams. Head still glued to the pillow, she wiggled her body backward to move closer to Eric. Desereé reached her destination and found herself rubbing on a body as soft as hers.

She sat straight up and scanned the room to be sure she was in the right suite. When her surroundings came into view, she saw a silk gold-toned love chair for two. Desereé's black satin gown lay on the arm of the chair, and her Jimmy Choo strapped shoes were on the floor below it. Her and Eric's luggage sat in the corner still unpacked. It was confirmed that the room was indeed hers, but where was Eric? And who was in their bed?

Afraid to face reality, Deseree turned slowly toward the soft body. There lay a petite beauty with skin like bronze and soft tresses that fell over her face as she slept.

What the hell did I get myself into, and where is Eric?

Feeling like she had been hit by a train, Deseree slid out of the bed and headed for the shower.

Deseree Nicole Parker was a five-foot-nine cutie that had the whole package, brains and beauty. She was a fair-skinned African American girl who was often mistaken for a biracial beauty. Her shoulder-length, chestnut brown, curly hair and alluring eyes could hypnotize any lover in her view. A middle child, she always struggled to be the best at everything to gain some recognition. As the only girl, she also yearned for the female companionship that only a sister could give. With her exotic look and an uncertain place in her world, she struggled with resentment as a result of people who accused her of being another race. She would always say, "Black comes in all shades! I'm one hundred percent black and proud of it!" Most people who received this response from her were the ignorant ones who thought telling her that she looked mixed was a compliment.

Deseree was a professional powerhouse and the brains behind the firm Parker, Lietum, and Gross. At thirty-two years old, she was sharp and the lifeline of her company. Deseree worked as a Forensic Lawyer at a firm that she helped build from the ground up. She was given the title due to her sharp analytical skills and attention to detail. She always provided accurate, timely, and thorough information to all levels of her cases. However, this gift sometimes eluded her in her personal life.

Dereseé tiptoed her way to the bathroom that was a ways away in the oversized suite. She had no luck finding Eric along the way. When she got closer to the bathroom, she heard muffled conversation coming from within.

Great. Now Eric can explain to me what's going on and why I feel drugged.

Dereseé opened the bathroom door and what she saw shook her to her core. Eric stood in the shower, but he was not alone. The muffled sounds she heard only moments ago were of them moaning and grunting. The water ran slowly down Eric's back as he moved his hips methodically with each stroke. Facing him was an unidentified man who had the body of a swimmer, lean and cut. Dereseé's mouth fell open. Suddenly, a tall, shapely women rose up from a doggy style position and faced Eric so he could take her from the front. Her skin was smooth like porcelain, and her curly red hair fell in her face as she wrapped her legs around Eric and mounted him while releasing a loud moan.

Dereseé eased out of the door and closed it behind her. What she thought was a sexy dream really happened. Seeing the red-headed lady who she had played with in her dream confirmed it. Dereseé had just been reminded that she and Eric had really gone too far. She leaned against the door, resting her head against the left side of the doorframe as it all came back to her.

Dereseé walked briskly toward the front of the suite. She stopped, stumbled forward, and almost landed on the floor.

After checking her right foot for blood, she examined the area for the culprit that tripped her. There lay a pair of red stilettos, reminding her of the beauty sleeping in her and Eric's bed.

Once satisfied with her examination, she hurried on, grabbing her purse along the way. Dereseé slid inside of the spacious closet in the living room area. She breathed heavily, and her hands shook as she searched for her cell phone in her purse. She could hear voices from the bathroom and wanted to hurry to make her lifeline call before Eric and the others found her. Finally finding her cell phone, Dereseé dialed the number two on her speed dial.

"Shit, Michelle, please pick up," she whispered with urgency in her voice.

The phone just rang. Dereseé could hear footsteps approaching the closet. She tried to leave a quick message while speaking softly. She needed her friend more than ever before; she was obviously in over her head. Before she could finish her message, the footsteps stopped in front of the closet and the door swung open.

Mistress Micki

Two-Faced

Michelle, aka Mistress Micki, paced the floor, giving her subject the stare of death. She leaned in close to his face and began to speak.

"What's my name, you lowdown maggot? Answer me, slave! Drop down to your knees and show me some respect!"

As the last word escaped her lips, the sound of her cell phone ringing blared from her purse. She had forgotten to turn it on silent mode. Micki strutted across the room to retrieve her phone. Her subject looked up at her, which made her furious. She hurried from silencing her phone and met him with furry.

Mistress Micki stood face to face with her subject, Bill, in her large studio-style apartment located in a renovated warehouse she rented for her encounters with her johns. Mistress Micki was always down for whatever as long as the money was green. She often preferred playing the Dominatrix role. It gave her a rush to inflict pain on whosoever was willing and able to withstand it.

She stood over Bill with authority, waving her favorite bullwhip with the iced out handle. With just a slight flick of her wrist, she cracked the whip, striking him in the middle of his back and sending signals of intense pain throughout his body. Bill jumped slightly. Then, his member stiffened. He humbly dropped his head and slowly crawled toward her on his knees.

"I beg you...please accept my apology, Mistress. It was never my intention to disrespect you," Bill's voice quivered. "My wife—"

"Your wife is not my problem!" Mistress Micki interrupted. "On Tuesdays at six o'clock a.m., I'm your wife, boy! Do you understand me?"

"Yes, Mistress," Bill replied cowardly.

Mistress Micki paused for a moment and then said, "Since this is your first offense, I'll forgive you, slave. Now assume the position, bitch!"

Bill could still feel the stinging across his back from the whip as he dropped to his hands and knees like a dog. He was dressed in nothing but a leather mask. Bill, a very rich man, had a sick fetish for pain. Unfortunately, his wife was not down with the same program. So, he ventured out to find someone whose cold and callous torture could make him explode.

Micki was a woman who had an insatiable desire to do whatever necessary to fulfill a man's erotic fantasy. When Bill found Micki through a social dating site, he struck gold. She did things to him that could be considered illegal in every corner of the world.

Every Tuesday at six o'clock in the morning, he had an appointment to be verbally and physically abused by a beautiful vixen who knew how to inflict the kind of pain that made his magic wand grow.

Mistress Micki walked over to a large closet where she kept all of her favorite toys. It looked like something out of the *Little Shop of Horrors.* She stared into the closet for about twenty seconds, contemplating how she was going to make this session one of few memorable moments in Bill's life that he would never forget. She finally reached for a dog collar with a long leather leash, a pair of fuzzy, black handcuffs, a riding crop, a cat-o-nine tails whip, and a pair of nipple clamps. She placed them on a table close to her subject while he remained motionless in the center of the floor. Picking up the riding crop, she ran her fingers up and down the shaft as her mouth formed a sinister grin. She thought to herself, *Oh yeah, this is perfect.*

Mistress Micki turned her attention back to Bill. She walked around his plump, naked body slowly, gently hitting the leather tongue on the palm of her hand as she inspected every inch. Bill was not the kind of guy Micki would have wanted for herself as far as looks were concerned. However, if he were to offer to take care of her for the rest of her natural born life, she would definitely consider looking past her desires for a sexy, muscular man that could beat up her uterus, and instead settle for a chubby millionaire who couldn't get it up unless he was getting beat up.

Bill could hear her eight-inch, leather stiletto boots as they clicked against the shiny hardwood floor behind him.

After a period of silence, Mistress Micki calmly said, "You know, lateness is not and will not be tolerated. When you don't show up on time, that is blatant disrespect, and you should be punished. My time is valuable, and I'm not about to share it with anyone or anything. You understand me, bitch?"

"Yes, Mistress," Bill replied.

Her subject's knees began to burn from being pressed against the hard wood.

Feeling a little merciful, Mistress Micki said, "Alright, slave, I will let you off with a warning this time. But, let that shit happen again and you will suffer my wrath."

"Thank you, Mistress," Bill responded.

Mistress Micki wore a matching leather thong and bra with spikes that covered both cups. She slowly raised one leg in the air and carefully placed her foot on Bill's shoulder, exposing the wet jewel between her legs. Bill began to salivate. Never had he met a woman so beautiful, flexible, and aggressive. He often contemplated leaving his wife just so he could be with Micki, but he knew that would take the fun out of his fantasies. Besides, there was no way Micki would give up her freedom to be on lockdown for just one man.

"Now, be a good boy and clean my boot," Mistress Micki ordered.

Without hesitation, Bill took his tongue and gently ran it across the tip of her boot like a paintbrush. He uttered moans of sexual pleasure while licking her boot clean. Mistress Micki draped her entire leg across Bill's shoulder so his nose met her sensual essence as it dripped nectar. She watched him enjoy her torturous acts. Although he wanted to extend his tongue forward and plunge it into her tunnel, he remained still. He knew if he made any moves without permission, there would be hell to pay. Mistress Micki raised the riding crop and swung it forcefully yet slowly, hitting each butt cheek five times. The more she hit him, the more excited he became.

"You like that?" Mistress Micki asked in a soft, sensuous growl.

"Yes, Mistress."

"You want more?"

"Yes, Mistress."

Mistress Micki dropped her leg and stood in front of her subject looking down on him like a giant.

"Very good, slave," Micki said with approval.

Mistress Micki grabbed a folding chair from a nearby corner and brought it to the center of the floor. She sat down slowly. As she slid her booty toward the edge of the chair, she spread her legs wide open.

"Now, please me. If you do a good job, I will reward you handsomely."

Mistress Micki took the collar with leash and hooked it to Bill's neck. She yanked it once and whistled.

"Here, doggie!" Mistress Micki bellowed softly.

Still in a kneeling position, Bill crawled over toward his mistress, who bound him with handcuffs. She tightened up on the leash, pulling him down on his hands and knees like a dog. She grabbed the long, blonde ponytail that hung from the back of the mask and pulled him forward, right between her legs.

"It's dinnertime," Mistress Micki said, smiling.

The subject's tongue emerged from the opening of the mask and gently moved the leather covering that hid her neatly shaven treasure chest to the side. His tongue plunged deep inside her as she exhaled. She began moving her hips in a circular motion, causing his tongue to move in and out of her erotic zone. She took the riding crop and began spanking him, which caused his tongue to quicken its pace. As Mistress Micki felt herself about to explode, she abruptly stopped him.

"Did I do something wrong, Mistress?" her subject asked.

"Did I give you permission to speak, slave?" Mistress Micki said harshly.

"No, Mistress," the subject replied in a submissive tone.

Mistress Micki got up. She walked behind him, took her boot, and pressed it against the small of Bill's back as she guided her heel between his cheeks, directly into the hole. His body tightened to keep from yelling out loud.

"Next time, only speak when you are spoken to. Do you understand, slave?"

"Yes, Mistress."

Mistress Micki reached for the el she rolled earlier just for the occasion. She lit it, took a long drag, and blew the smoke right in his face.

"Stick out your tongue," Mistress Micki said, and Bill complied.

She hit the el, causing the ash that hung from it to fall on Bill's tongue.

"Now, eat it," Mistress Micki demanded.

Bill swallowed the ash like it was the tastiest delicacy he ever had. Mistress Micki did this at least two more times, leaving his tongue red and sore. As the buzz from the weed set in, Mistress Micki reached for the cat-o-nine tails whip off the table. She gripped it tightly and gave him three lashes across the back, producing red welts across his white skin. Then she made him get up off the floor. As he stood to his feet, Mistress Micki was greeted with a rock-hard shaft.

Damn! Not bad, she thought to herself. *If I were insane, I'd mount that and give him a lap dance he'll never forget!*

Bill longed for the day when Mistress Micki would actually allow him to enter her walls with his member instead of just his tongue. But, it was Mistress Micki's show, and until she gave her approval, he had to settle for the painful pleasure that kept him coming back every week.

Still standing behind him and holding on to the leash, Mistress Micki grabbed his manhood and began stroking the shaft. Bill stood defenseless while she moved her hand from the tip to the base in a circular motion. The faster she stroked, the faster he breathed. Noticing her subject was about to reach his peak, Mistress Micki grabbed the riding crop again and gave him a lick right below his scrotum. His heart beat wildly against his chest. He couldn't take it any longer.

When Mistress Micki realized her subject was about to blow his load, she reached down inside her bra and pulled out a syringe filled with a small dose of adrenaline to give him a high that would send his mind to the moon. At the precise time, Mistress Micki jabbed the needle into the side of his neck. The subject's eyes grew wide as the drugs penetrated his muscles. His heart raced and beads of sweat formed on his brow. Then, his body convulsed with a mind-blowing intensity that was unlike anything he'd ever felt before. It was as if he were having an out-of-body experience.

His creamy fluid flowed from his body like the Nile River. Mistress Micki held her head under the tip of his manhood as if it were the faucet and her mouth were the sink. As his juices flowed downward, Mistress Micki caught every drop in her mouth. Bill grew weak as his fluids left his body. He tried to regain his composure, but he collapsed to the floor like a rag doll.

Mistress Micki spit his liquid out of her mouth onto his jiggly, naked body. She then stepped over Bill and went to the bathroom to wash. When she returned, she found Bill still lying on the floor. She checked his vital signs before removing the handcuffs.

"I have no more use for you. Leave me," she said coldly.

Bill rose unsteadily to his feet and stumbled over to the chair where his clothes lie. His eyes still wide, he watched as his hands shook uncontrollably. His heart continued to race from the drugs. He reached into his pants pocket and pulled out a gold money clip filled with crisp one-hundred-dollar bills. He removed the clip, peeled off three thousand dollars, and left it on the table where her toys sat. While she was in the kitchen pouring herself a glass of wine, Bill got dressed and departed Mistress Micki's domain without uttering a single word.

Mistress Micki looked at her clock, which read 8:30 a.m. *Oh shit, I've got to be at work at eleven o'clock. Let me get my ass home,* she thought. She cleaned up all that remained from the session, gathered her belongings, and headed home to transform for her day job.

Desereé

Undercover

Curled up in a fetal position, Desereé crouched inside the closet broken from the past night's events and the fact that her friend was not available. She held her breath hoping the person on the other side of the door would pass by. With no luck, she heard the closet door being manipulated.

"Please don't let them open this door," she whispered, panicking.

Her plead went unanswered. The door to the closet flew open, allowing the light from the room to stream in the dark space. Desereé looked up and saw Eric standing there with his natural skin exposed from his feet up to his head. He stared down at Desereé with his head tilted to the left side. No words were exchanged for a moment. Then Eric broke the silence.

"Babe, what are you doing in the closet and who were you talking to? I've been looking for you since I got out of the shower."

Dereseé stared at him with molten balls. She burned holes in his flesh with her stare.

"Do you mean once y'all got out of the shower! Eric, who the hell are you? This trip was a mistake! What the hell are you into?"

Dereseé stared at the man who she had known for over eight years and could not recognize who he had become. Now in a stance of power, she arose from her fetal position and pushed past Eric, heading for the bedroom. Not saying a word, Eric followed behind her trying to do damage control. He reached his hand out to grab her arm.

"Baby, wait. I'm sorry you had to see that. I tried to wait for you to get up, but things just spun out of control."

Dereseé was prepared to start whipping some ass and put everyone out of their room, but as she approached the bedroom, she saw the company had left. She grabbed her suitcase and stormed over to the dresser, grabbing her toiletries from the top first.

"Babe, where are you going? Wait, we still have some days left here. You agreed."

Dereseé had enough. She turned to face him, hand on her hip as she stared him right in his eyes.

"Eric, you've lost your complete mind. I agreed to a little kinkiness with my husband, not an all-out freak show for days. I wake up with a woman in my bed who I don't even remember being with, and then find my husband in the shower screwing some other hoe with a strange man. Eric, this is not what I signed up for! And since when have you been so freaky? What I saw this morning was that of a pro-freak, not an amateur."

In a frenzy, Deseré did not let Eric respond. She went from packing toiletries to clothes as she stormed through the room.

"Oh, you have nothing to say?" she said.

Eric stood in one spot not really knowing how to respond. For the first time since he stepped foot on the campus of Villanova Law School, he was at a loss for words. The truth is he had been freaking for about three months and was addicted to the level of sexual pleasure he had been missing in his relationship. He couldn't tell his wife all of his secrets, at least not yet. Eric mustered up some balls with a play for sympathy and broke his silence with such meager words for a wordsmith.

"I'm sorry, D. I feel horrible that I brought you into this."

Deseré wasn't buying his act. He forgot she could read body language and assess a situation with her eyes closed.

"My ass, you are not sorry, and I have reason to believe I was drugged last night. The events are real foggy, and my head feels funny."

Deseré attempted to stay in her strong voice, but started to break down. The thought of her husband drugging her for freak sex evoked sorrow deep from within. Tears rolled down her face like a gushing river. She struggled to speak in between sobs.

"How could you do this to me, Eric…to us? This ain't right. It just ain't right."

With her luggage packed, a now fully dressed Deseré attempted to walk past Eric while wiping her tears. Eric became agitated and his whole demeanor changed. He stood in front of Dereseé, blocking the doorway.

"Now hold up, Dessie! You're not going to blame all of this on me. You agreed to come to a swingers' retreat! What did you think we were going to do, hold hands? Grow up. This is the real world that we live in, and no one held you here against your will. I'm sorry if you seeing me with another woman was sobering, but that's what we both signed up for the moment we agreed to come. From my memory, you enjoyed three guys last night and the girl you woke up with. So, if you want to go, then leave, but don't blame anyone for your choices."

Eric was in full lawyer mode as he performed for his invisible jury. He took a deep breath and hit his broad chiseled chest as he continued.

"We were in this together, remember? But, I have no problem finishing alone. We paid a lot of money to be here and took a lot of time to make this decision, but if you're leaving, I will see you in a few days."

Eric stepped to the side, clearing the path of freedom for Dereseé to exit. Dereseé did just that without giving any closing arguments. She pulled her suitcase as she headed toward the elevator with tear-filled eyes. Dereseé stood at the massive golden elevator doors awaiting the red light to stop on her floor. The tears were uncontrollable. She had no idea what had just happened and why. Dereseé attempted to reach Michelle by phone once more with no luck. She not only needed her friend for support, but also for a ride out of hell. Once Dereseé didn't get her, she knew she needed a Plan B since she could not go back in there with Eric.

The elevator arrived, and Dereseé hurried on before getting caught in the doors. Once inside, she sat her purse on top of her luggage and began searching her cell phone for lifelines. Dereseé didn't want anyone in her business. So, she sought long and hard for the right person for the job. She came across Sanai's number, but then thought twice about it. Sanai and she were cool; however, she did not want this fiasco to end up the next topic at "cocktales night".

As she reached the lobby, her phone rang and erased the message she had been writing. Dereseé struggled to get off of the elevator. When she checked the caller ID, her eyes went wide trying to be sure the number was correct. The name Chance scrolled across her screen and caused butterflies in her gut. Dereseé knew answering the call could be a bad move, but she was desperate and knew Chance would not mind driving a few hours from the city to pick her up.

"Hello. Dessie speaking."

"Hello, beautiful. How are you?"

Dereseé leaned against the lobby wall, getting comfortable. His smooth voice brought back many memories.

"I'm okay, but in a bit of a bind right now," she threw out there just to see where he would go with it.

Chance cleared his throat. "A bind? What sort of bind? I know we haven't spoken in a long while, but I do still care about you. A bind for you is one for me."

"Is that right, Mr. Chance?"

Dereseé had not spoken to him since Eric made her fire him due to his fondness for her when he worked as a paralegal for his internship. Dereseé had to think fast.

"Well, I'm on a getaway to clear my head from the stress of working, and my car broke down. To make matters worse, Eric is away on business, and I'm due back in town today for this big case I'm prepping for."

Chance listened, then responded as he tapped his pen on his desk. "Well, I guess I have perfect timing then. I was calling to ask you out for lunch. I have something I want to discuss with you. I can always come pick you up. Where are you?"

Deseré hesitated. "I could not take you out of your way like that. I'm a few hours out of the city. Well, about two and a half hours to be exact."

"That's not too far. I can pick you up and have you back where you belong in no time," Chance insisted.

Deseré placed him on hold while she got the address of the nearest mall and restaurant area. She held the paper containing the information and proceeded to tell him, "Okay, Chance, I'm back. You can meet me at Cottage Chateau in about two hours. That way, we can do lunch before we get on the road. Don't be late, because the hotel shuttle is prompt. It will get me there on time, and I don't want to look like I was stood up."

The pair shared a laugh before hanging up. Deseré had no idea what she would do for the next two hours to pass the time, but she knew she did not want to see Eric. So, Deseré headed to the hotel lounge to devise a plan.

Michelle

Chance Encounter

Micki awakened to birds chirping from the trees outside the window of her condo. The sun was shining and a warm breeze rippled through the curtains of her bedroom window. She enjoyed waking to such a beautiful scene. It always seemed to rejuvenate her. Micki rose from her bed feeling refreshed and ready to take on another day.

Dr. Michelle Jacobs a.k.a. Micki was a successful doctor who worked tirelessly day in and day out as one of the senior physicians on staff in the emergency room at Abington Hospital. She had seen all types of emergency cases. No matter what condition came through the door, she was ready. From gunshots and stabbings to the birth of a baby, she always rose to the occasion.

Ever since she was a young girl, Micki had been an action junkie. She found things most people would consider insane or disgusting to be intriguing. Knowing she held the fate of her patients in her hands gave Micki a rush that made her wet with excitement. Some of the drama she had to deal with on a daily basis would make the average person sick. Nevertheless, she found her job more adventurous and unpredictable than a one-night stand.

Micki didn't need for anything. Her career as a doctor paid very well. For some reason, that just wasn't enough, though. Micki wanted and needed more. So, in addition to her demanding medical career, Micki moonlighted as a personal escort, which was her professional term for a prostitute. Her cousin, Tisha, introduced her to the profession when she was struggling through medical school. Tisha always showed up at family functions wearing the hottest designs money could buy. Rumors circulated around the family about Tisha's many boyfriends, her spending habits, and her tribe of children who were spread out among family members across the city due to her many mysterious disappearances that she often disguised as business trips.

One day, Micki decided to put all the rumors to bed and ask her straight up about how she made her cash. Micki was tired of struggling to pay her bills. With a hefty tuition bill, she had to find some way of making extra money to keep her head above water. When Micki's cousin shared about her line of work, her eyes stretched wide as she anticipated hearing more. From what Micki was told, she had the ability to make a lot of money. To make money with little effort, Micki was down for whatever.

At first, Micki started out doing some small parties with her cousin for which she got paid well. Then, Micki began establishing her own clientele, which brought in about two thousand tax-free dollars weekly. Micki vowed to stop her extracurricular activities after she graduated from medical school, finished her residency, and got a job, but when she saw how well the extra paper catered to her lavish lifestyle, she couldn't let it go. She figured it was just another adventure for the record books.

Micki dabbled in a little bit of everything. From innocent foreplay to S&M, she was willing to do anything as long as the price was right. Micki lived her life on the edge, and she wouldn't want it any other way. She was very careful to make sure what she did in the dark never saw daylight. Not even her closest friends Sanai, Layla, and Desereé knew how she spent her free time outside of their monthly girls' night out for drinks, while sharing their crazy sex stories and flirting with the waiters who served them.

Micki arrived for her shift at exactly seven o'clock in the morning. It was a Friday, and she was ready to get her workday started and over with. Before they clocked out, the night staff briefed her about the patients. While walking around the floor making her rounds, she came across a young man who had been brought in just before she arrived for her shift. A bandage on his cheek covered a wound that was once a gaping hole left by a bullet. The man lay in the bed like a zombie, staring off into space with large puddles forming in his tear ducts.

Micki reviewed her notes from her conference with the night staff, then raised one eyebrow. She learned the gunshot wound was the result of a botched suicide attempt. The patient had inserted a gun in his mouth and aimed at the back of his throat. While the man had his finger on the trigger ready to fire, someone busted through his bedroom door and tripped on a huge box sitting in the middle of the floor, causing him to fall into the man's arm that shifted the gun in the direction of his cheek. It turned out that the divine presence of a clumsy family member horsing around in the house saved the man from splattering his brains all over the walls of his bedroom.

Micki looked at his birth date, and to her surprise, he was born in 1992. She shook her head. He was only twenty years old. *What is so bad in this boy's life that would make him want to take himself out?* Micki thought to herself.

She scrolled the chart further and found a possible explanation. Judging from the blank expression on his face, he was not happy about how things turned out. She tucked away her emotions and entered the room.

"Good morning, Mr. Davis. I'm Dr. Jacobs. I just wanted to stop by, check you out, and see how you're feeling." Micki tried to sound as cheerful as she could considering the circumstances, but even she wasn't convinced her attempt was believable.

Trevor Davis slowly turned his head in her direction. As he gazed toward her with tired, hopeless eyes, the tears began to flow.

"How can I help you, Mr. Davis?" Micki asked.

The pain medication had him feeling no pain, but the reality of his situation was enough for him to want to end his life.

"Everything would have been fine if they had just let me bleed to death!" Trevor responded in a slurred tone. "I'm such a dumb ass! I should have prepared better. I knew my dumb-ass cousin was running around the house acting like a fool. I should've locked my door."

Micki had to work hard not to react impulsively to what she'd just heard.

In a calm voice, she replied, "I'm sorry you felt your life was so bad that you had to resort to ending it. I'm not a psychiatrist, but I can make a referral if you would like to talk to someone."

"I don't want to talk to anyone! Isn't it obvious? I don't want to be here! You might as well say my life is over. I lost my true love forever, and now, it's just a matter of time before I lose everything, including my life…all because that bitch wanted to have his cake and eat it, too!"

A blanket of tears blinded Trevor's eyes as he reached for Micki's stethoscope that hung around her neck.

Awww shit! Micki thought as she took a step backwards to avoid his reach. In situations like these, she had to constantly remind herself she was in the helping profession, because for a brief moment, her comforting, bedside manner almost went out the window. Without thought, she fell back into a fighting stance ready to deliver a clear shot right to his eye. She caught herself and rang for the orderlies to come strap him down. Then, she called to the charge nurse.

"Get the crisis unit on the phone and see if they can get a bed for this patient, stat! He needs to be placed under suicide watch for seventy-two hours and given a psychiatric evaluation."

After the staff sprang into action, Micki updated Trevor's chart quickly.

Damn! Being HIV positive can make people do some really crazy shit! If this day continues like this, I may need a drink before my shift ends, Micki mumbled to herself, then

shook her head and moved on to her next patient.

After two hours of visiting patients, Micki went to her office to update her patient notes. Although she enjoyed the events of the morning, she would have been better prepared to handle them had she'd been able to have her morning cup of coffee first. Unfortunately, the coffee machine was down. So, she had to wait for a break to grab a cup from the cafeteria.

Micki felt the subtle vibration of her cell phone against her hip. She pulled it out of its case and took a look. A yellow envelope icon appeared in the upper left corner of her screen. Looking at her phone reminded her that she never called Dereseé back. It was a text message from Sani, which read, "Hey, bitches! This is a reminder about our monthly girls' night out at RUMBAR. It has been changed to Positano Coast in Old City next Friday at 8 p.m. sharp. Get ready for cocktales and refreshments!"

Micki giggled at the sight of the word "cocktales". Dereseé coined the term years ago to describe the steamy stories told over drinks at their monthly girls' night out. Micki's excitement about the text gave her a renewed energy. Although it was about a week away, she still was eager. It was almost the type of energy she felt right before putting her thing down on one of her customers. It wasn't often she got to hang out with her girls eating, drinking, and sharing some of the craziest stories known to man. Micki shared a few stories, but none of them were even close to the crazy mess she got into in her other life.

She shuffled her papers around and began to write her patient notes. As she reached across the desk to grab her water, she accidentally pushed all of the files she had to work on to the floor.

"My crazy morning just keeps on giving," she said aloud while retrieving the papers from the floor. Micki jerked her right hand back and yelled, "Damn!"

Her right index finger was bleeding from a paper cut. As Micki administered first aid to her finger, she gazed at the personal information form of the file now on top. The name of the patient's place of employment read Parker, Lietum, and Gross Law Firm, which caught her eye.

Micki finished nursing her cut and opened the file for further investigation. Leaning back in her comfy chair, she scanned the pages, computing information like a robot. She was searching for Mr. Trevor Davis' list of lovers for the past two years so they could be contacted and encouraged to get tested. She came across the form and noticed only two names were scribbled on the form. Micki felt really bad that this kid with a limited sexual history was now infected with HIV.

As she read it closely and tried to make the second name out, she mouthed the letters E…P…I. Micki held it closer to her face and then dropped the paper as her heart beat with force against her chest wall. The second letter was in clear view.

"R… Noooo!" she yelled.

Letting the words drag out slowly, Micki connected the dots.

Layla

Caught Up

With her face implanted in her pillow, Layla's hands gripped the satin sheets as she received pelvic thrusts from her husband. Her back perfectly arched with his hands on her waist, she surrendered her pink walls while in his favorite position, letting his name slip out in between her moans.

"Oh, Darren…oh, Darren," she let out.

While pretending to enjoy every second of the sexual encounter, deep down, Layla's body craved the soft caresses from a certain someone ever since she shared her bed that special night. While her mind wandered to that special place, she could feel Darren ejaculating inside her. So, she decided to shiver a little bit, showing off her acting skills. The way she shook she could have won an Oscar convincing Darren that he was hitting her spot correctly. They both lay on their backs breathing heavily. Darren was the first to speak.

"I ain't have you shake like that in a while. I must've been hitting ya spot, babe."

"Yes, you were," Layla said with a smile as she rolled over and kissed him on the cheek.

"I hope you don't think it's over. Wait until we get in the shower," Darren told her, then popped up and went into the bathroom.

After she heard the water running, Layla lay on her back and returned to concentrating on that special someone. She fantasized that she was kissing, licking, and sucking her nipples. Then, she licked her fingers and guided them down to her clit. Surrendering to her thoughts, she began to satisfy herself until she started shaking authentically this time. After climaxing, she drifted off into a deep sleep, forgetting to make it into the shower for round two with Darren.

*****

Layla stood over the stove placing cheese on her scrambled eggs, the last addition to her breakfast that also included sausage and pancakes. Darren's footsteps could be heard as his shoes hit the marble floor as he walked over to kiss her on the neck. Her long, sandy brown hair lay perfectly against her mid back.

"Good morning, babe," he said after giving her a peck on her cheek where a cluster of freckles resided.

"Hey, babe," Layla replied, turning around with the non-stick pan and spatula to place the eggs on her plate.

Layla was caramel brown with chocolate freckles neatly about her nose and cheeks. She had almond-shaped eyes that were full of life and pretty plump lips.

"So what happened to you last night?" Darren asked, ending the brief silence.

"I'm sorry, babe. I didn't know I even dozed off," Layla answered, saying the first thing that came to her mind as she poured some orange juice.

"Well, don't let it happen again. I had to finish the second round without you."

Darren's words caused Layla to twist up her face and added some tension in the air, but their daughter running into the kitchen quickly killed it.

"Good morning, Mommy!" London yelled as she ran into her arms.

Layla hugged London, then put her down and kneeled to talk to her.

"What did I tell you about running in my kitchen?"

"Sorry, Mommy," London replied, feeling a little embarrassed.

After speaking to London, Layla looked over at Darren, who stood there burning a hole through her. By the look on his face, she knew he wanted to put closure to their conversation.

"London baby, go upstairs and get your book bag. Daddy is ready to take you to school."

London ran out of the kitchen and upstairs to her room. After hearing her reach the steps, Layla proceeded with their conversation.

"Look, I'm sorry, Darren. It won't happen again. I just have a lot on my mind, sweetie," she explained as she sat down to begin eating.

"All I'm saying is make that the last time. That was the third time it happened in the last month. One more time and it's going to be a problem," Darren warned before walking out the kitchen.

Layla threw her fork down, rose from her chair, and followed him while speaking at the same time.

"What's that supposed to mean?" Layla asked, then stopped in her tracks and put her hands on her hips.

Once again, the tension that rose was killed when London ran downstairs ready to go school. Darren went inside the closet and grabbed his briefcase, then opened the door.

"Give your mom a hug and kiss, London," he said, while holding the door open.

Layla kneeled down to receive London's daughterly love. After rising, she stood there waiting for Darren to walk over to give her some love, but instead, he waited until London walked out and then closed the door behind him.

"Whatever," Layla said out loud to herself as she walked back into the kitchen and sat down to finish her breakfast.

Darren's actions didn't help the fact that it was the twelve-year anniversary of when her brother was murdered. While eating, her thoughts were all over the place. She thought about how she had to get flowers for when she went to his gravesite, and then her mind traveled to her dilemma. The anxiety about it overwhelming, she had started writing her thoughts out to ease the anxiousness.

She quickly rose from the table and went upstairs to her closet. After moving a couple of shoeboxes, she grabbed the hidden red one. Upon opening it, she noticed what she came to get wasn't there. She panicked, but then remembered she had left her diary in her work desk. Her diary was therapeutic for her, allowing her to write her innermost thoughts. She also used it to jot down notes for the novel she was writing titled *B.F.F. (Best Friends Forever)*, which would be loosely based on her life. Being that she was a columnist for the *Daily News*, writing came naturally for her. She took a deep breath, knowing that was another stop she had to make since she wanted to use this day to finish up writing her novel.

Time was of the essence. So, she returned the box to its hiding place and then went back downstairs to finish eating. While eating, she received a text from Sanai stating what time she would be going to the gravesite. Sanai played a significant role in going to the gravesite. She had dated Layla's brother for years before his death, and that's how they met. Layla and Sanai clicked early on in their relationship. She was a big supporter of her brother and Sanai's relationship. Layla always proposed they should get married, but his life was taken before that could happen.

She texted Sanai back, informing her of everything she had on her itinerary, and then told her to meet her there by three o'clock that afternoon.

*****

After stopping past her workplace and the flower shop, Layla pulled up to the gravesite. Reaching over to the passenger seat, she grabbed the flowers, then stepped out of her black 2012 Maxima and walked over to her brother's final resting place. With every step she took, her emotions grew. By the time she reached his grave, tears were streaming down her cheeks. She placed the flowers by his tombstone that read: *Gone Too Soon, R.I.P. Lawrence "King" Phillips, Sunrise 12/12/79 - Sunset 7/4/2000.*

Layla wiped away her tears, took a deep breath, and went into a brief conversation.

"Hey, King, I just wanted to say I love you and I miss you."

After speaking those few words, she was interrupted by another car pulling up beside hers. It was Sanai arriving in her X6. She hopped out with flowers in her hand and walked over to where Layla was standing. As she approached, the Chanel shades she wore couldn't hide the tears streaming down her face. She gave her best friend a hug before placing the flowers on the opposite side of where Layla had placed hers.

"Hey, girl, how you feeling?" Sanai asked through a couple of sniffles.

"I'm okay. Just had a brief conversation with King before you pulled up," Layla answered, then took a deep breath.

Sanai began looking around before speaking again.

"I don't know about you, but graveyards give me the creeps."

"Girl, you crazy," Layla replied with a chuckle. "But, I feel you. They're kinda scary, yet so quiet and peaceful," she added as she looked around, as well.

Wanting to break the somber moment, Sanai spoke up.

"Hey, let's quit with all this sadness. You know King wouldn't want us crying and everything. What you say we go to his favorite restaurant and grab a bite to eat and have a drink or two?"

Layla stood in thought and sighed before answering.

"You know what? You're right. Sounds like fun. Plus, with all this crying, a drink doesn't sound bad."

After paying their respects for yet another year, they both hopped in their cars and headed for their next destination.

*****

Pulling up to the Olive Garden on City Line Avenue, Layla and Sanai parked side by side. As they walked in, the sounds of Frank Sinatra could be heard coming from the speakers. There were only two people in line, and as they stood behind them waiting for their turn to be seated, Sanai turned to Layla, who was standing on her right, and began to speak.

"I'm glad we came now and not at lunchtime, 'cause we probably would've been waiting a half hour to be seated."

"I know, right? Plus, I hate when they give you that big-ass pager to hold," Layla responded.

Once the couple in front of them was seated, another hostess came and introduced herself. Then, she led them to a quiet location in the rear of the restaurant. Five minutes later, their waiter walked up.

"Hello, my name is Kelly, and I'll be your waitress. Are you two ready to order?"

Both Sanai and Layla told her no and to give them some time. However, they were ready to order their drinks.

"What type of drinks would you like to order?" Kelly asked, while looking in the direction of Sanai.

"I would like to order a glass of wine," Sanai replied as she looked over the drink menu.

Before she could finish, Kelly chimed in, "The wine of the day is the Sangria. Would you like to taste test?"

Sanai thought about it for a second and then answered, "No. I would like two glasses of White Zinfandel, one now and one when my food arrives."

Kelly wrote down Sanai's order before turning to Layla.

"I would like two glasses of Moscato, one now and the other when my food arrives."

"Okay, I will be back with your drinks," Kelly said, then walked away.

Layla sat back and stared out the window. Normally, she would be the one starting a conversation. Sanai received a text. Once she replied to the message, she spoke on Layla being so quiet.

"What's up, girl? You're not acting like yourself today. Is something bothering you?"

Layla sat up and put both her forearms on the table. "Besides thinking about King, I'm okay."

Sanai smiled and decided to cheer her friend up with nostalgia.

"Remember the first time he brought us here? We were only eighteen and he knew the waitress. We got so drunk and were laughing so loud that the manager kicked us out."

Sanai and Layla began laughing hard at the thought. Their laughter caused a couple of patrons to look over in their direction, but they weren't paying them any attention.

"Oh my God, yes. Those were the good ole days," Layla said with a big smile on her face.

Kelly returned with their wine and then asked if they were ready to order.

"Yes, I would like to order the Tour de France, but could you put my order in a to-go box and cancel that second glass of wine," Sanai said, then went back to texting.

"Yes, no problem, and what about you, ma'am? What would you like to order?"

Ignoring the waitress, Layla screwed up her face, becoming instantly appalled at the fact her best friend seemed to be fleeing her.

"How could you just leave me like this? I thought we were supposed to be having a good time."

After Layla spoke, she grabbed her glass of wine, sat back, and sipped from the glass.

Kelly sensed the tension rising, so she decided she would come back. "I will come back to take your order, ma'am," she said, then stepped off to put in Sanai's order.

Sanai waited until Kelly walked away before responding.

"What's your problem? Look, something came up that I have to attend to at the moment. Oh, and could you handle the money deposit today after you collect from the stylists?"

Layla, who was staring out the window, turned to her friend of fourteen years with a look that would have gotten her fifteen years behind bars.

"Is the dick that good you have to leave me on a day like this?"

Sanai took a deep breath, exhaled, and then took a sip of her wine. "Look, I know you're having a rough day, but trust and believe, I would never put something such as that before you, especially on a day like this."

"Whatever. So who is that you're texting?" Layla inquired, pointing to Sanai's phone that was sitting on the table.

Right when she asked, Sanai's phone began vibrating again. Sanai grabbed her phone and began answering the text. After texting, she put the phone back down and looked up at Layla, who was still giving her the grizzly look while waiting for her answer.

"Look, girl, you're tripping right now. I know your emotions are a little out of whack today, but don't let them get the best of you."

Layla waved off Sanai with her right hand and blew out her breath. Then, she sat back and enjoyed her last couple of sips of wine while staring out the window as if Sanai wasn't sitting across from her. Sanai shook her head at the sight of her best friend lost in her emotions. She didn't comment; she just sipped her wine and enjoyed the strange silence.

Kelly walked up with Sanai's food and inquired about Layla.

"Are still looking to order, ma'am?"

Layla ignored Kelly's question as she continued to look out the window.

"No, Kelly, she's not ordering anything," Sanai answered for Layla. Then, she went into her purse to grab her Visa card and a ten-dollar bill.

"There you go, Kelly. That's your tip, and I will be taking care of the payment with that. The drinks are on me," Sanai added in a smart way directed towards Layla.

Kelly thanked her before walking off to process the payment. In about two minutes, she returned with Sanai's receipt. As soon as Sanai got up, Layla followed suite, and they both walked out together. Once outside and walking to their cars, Sanai reminded her about business.

"Look, girl, stop pouting, and don't forget to handle business. I will holla at you later," Sanai said as she gave her best friend a hug.

Layla hugged her back. Sanai could feel it wasn't as genuine as hers due to Layla holding a grudge.

"Whatever," Layla responded before they both got in their cars.

Layla waited until Sanai drove off first because she wanted to see which direction she was going in and then follow her. Sanai sat at the light with her left signal on, waiting to exit the plaza. Wanting to remain incognito and not make it obvious that she was following her, Layla drove up once she saw a car in back of Sanai. Once Sanai made a left onto City Line Avenue, the first light turned yellow, and she sped up to make it. Layla tried to make it, too; however, the car she was behind made it impossible. So, she just sat at the light trying to get a glance of what direction Sanai went, but she lost her in the slight traffic. Hitting the steering wheel, she decided to just drive to the salon and make the deposit.

Sanai

Lights, Camera, Action

Sanai stepped out her brand-new whirlpool feeling like a million bucks and slipped into her pink terrycloth bathrobe. She then walked over to her vanity set. One would think she was a Hollywood actress by the way it was setup. She even had the big light bulbs going around the frame. Let her tell it, she was Hollywood; she just didn't reside there.

Coming up as an only child, she was always taught the value of hard work, beginning with education. She graduated from Temple University, majoring in HealthCare Management and with a minor in Business Management. All that hard work resulted in Sanai owning a successful beauty/spa salon on City Line Avenue. She was also the Office Manager at the Penn Health System.

Sanai had success in her pocket, but lacked in the love department. This was due to her having three personalities that never seemed to help her be successful in both those areas of her life at the same time. One was the Boss Bitch persona, where she handled her business and didn't need any man to take care of her. The second persona was the Boss, where the bitch was absent; yet, she still wanted to control every situation. Last but not least was the Diva, where she would just flaunt her success and love to hang out with her girlfriends. Let her best friend Layla tell it, Sanai was all three everyday all day, but was too crazy to notice.

She never met a man worthy enough to give the title of boyfriend let alone husband. However, she was falling hard for a guy who she had been seeing for a few months. Her boss mentality would tell her to fuck them and let them go. There was one Sanai did want, but he was already taken. On the flip side, her boss bitch mentality made her say fuck it. As long as she was giving up the kitty and he bought her everything she wanted, she was okay with how things were going. This way of thinking and living made her one of the single ones out of the four-lady crew. Even her girlfriends were curious as to who was the cold-hearted bastard that made her this way, but the way Sanai saw it, she was born this way and would perish this way.

She came close to being with one man for life when she was younger, but he had his life snatched away from him, which sent her deeper into her single-for-life mode. Sanai was very adventurous and had a carefree attitude when it came to men. Her best friend Layla saw this as one of her strengths and adored Sanai for not compromising her feelings for the same "stick" day after day. She always knew when she wanted it and with whom. She even indulged in threesomes, but that was just her showing off her adventurous side. She never claimed to be bi-sexual; it was all in fun and trying new things out sexually.

After applying the finishing touches to her makeup, Sanai removed the silk Gucci rag from her wrapped hair. She then proceeded to press her hair with a flat iron. After the ten-minute pressing, she grabbed her favorite Bath and Body lotion and spray called Dark Kiss. This fragrance turned men on with its voluptuous berries, tempting blooms, and night musk. She put on the lotion before walking over to her walk-in closet to pick out a black all-purpose dress with the heels to match. She slipped into the dress and heels, then squirted the body spray over the dress to complement the scent of the lotion. Once she completed everything, she posed in front of the closet mirror to see if anything was missing. Looking closely, she realized she almost forgot one accessory, her Mac lip-gloss.

It was Friday night and Sanai was ready to hit the town. She applied the gloss to her lips and then puckered up at her reflection in the mirror, completing her beautification process. It was right on time, because at that moment, her phone signaled she had received a text stating her date wanted her to be at the Cuba Libre Restaurant in Old City at seven o'clock.

After reading the text message, Sanai hit the compose button on her cell phone. She had to send her second reminder to the girls about Cocktales at Positano Coast, which was exactly one week away. Michelle had been the only one to respond to the text she sent two days prior. After she doubled checked that she had included everyone on the text, she hit send. Then she grabbed her car keys and Kate Spade clutch before proceeding out the door.

Sanai arrived at her destination right on time. While driving, she thought she was being followed, which resulted in her becoming a little on edge. So, when she stepped out her car, she surveyed the area, fed the meter, and then entered the establishment. She had never been there before. However, it was her date's favorite spot, and he decided it would be a perfect place to dine out. He had some making up to do since their last encounter and argument.

As she walked in, she was in awe at the Cuban-styled restaurant. Tall palm trees graced the floors, while large ceiling fans hovered above her. The décor made Sanai feel as though she was in Cuba for a minute. That is until the hostess spoke and brought her back to reality.

"Welcome to Cuba Libre. Table for one or are you meeting someone?"

Just as the hostess finished greeting Sanai, her date walked in and informed the hostess that they had reservations. They were seated in a nice secluded area in the restaurant; the dim lighting set the mood for a very romantic evening.

The waitress came over promptly, introducing herself and then running down the food and drink specials while handing them the menus.

"Yes, I would like to order two Mojitos for me and my lovely date," Sanai's date ordered in a confident manner.

Sanai blushed at the compliment and then proceeded to place her order.

"I'm hungry. So, can we order the food now?"

"Sure. What will you be having this evening?" the waitress asked, focusing her attention on Sanai.

Sanai glanced over the menu again and finally decided what she wanted. Not wanting to mispronounce the order, she paused for a moment, took a deep breath, and then let it out.

"I would like the Arooz con Pollo meal, please."

"Arroz con Pollo," the waitress replied, correcting Sanai.

Sanai shot her a dirty look as if to say, *Bitch I'm not Cuban, so why are you correcting me?* She wanted to say something, but chose to bite her tongue; she didn't want to put a damper on the evening.

The waitress promptly wrote down Sanai's order, then turned to her date and asked, "And for you, sir?"

"I would like to order the Camornes on Cana."

With it being his favorite restaurant, the words flowed off his tongue like he spoke fluent Cuban.

"Would you like any water before I bring out your order of Mojitos?"

"No," they answered before the waitress walked off to put in their order.

"I see why this is your favorite restaurant. The customer service is excellent," Sanai said sarcastically, still a little irritated at the way the waitress corrected her.

"Yes, it is," her date replied, not picking up on her sarcasm. "I never leave here without giving a respectable tip. By the way, you look great and smell even better. What's that fragrance you're wearing?"

"It's called Dark Kiss by Bath and Body works. I have on the lotion and body spray."

"I'm impressed. I don't want it dark, but I hope I will be receiving a kiss at the end of our date."

"You can get whatever you want. Just don't want your wife to find out."

Sanai's statement made him chuckle.

"If my wife knew about us, I wouldn't be here."

"Well, let's hope she never finds out," Sanai said sincerely.

After the quick conversation between the two, the waitress brought over their drinks. Fifteen minutes later, she returned with their food and left them alone to enjoy their dinner and conversation. By the third drink, things began to get a little steamy as Sanai started feeling the effects from the alcohol.

"So now that we're done eating, what's next?"

Her date chuckled and answered, "What would you like to do? Your wish is my command."

"I like the sound of that. How about you take me outside in your truck?"

Sanai's date quickly called for the waitress, paid the bill, and left a fifty-dollar tip. They proceeded to end their night inside his Lincoln Navigator. Before they could make it outside, the waitress ran after Sanai's date to give him the money he left, not knowing it was her tip.

"Hey, Mister, you forgot your change," the waitress said, almost out of breath after running up on him.

"No, that's yours. I used to be a waiter, and I know how important tips are to one's survival."

"Thank you," the waitress said, while smiling and stuffing the hefty tip in her pocket.

"That was nice of you. Now let me give you a special tip," Sanai said seductively as they walked out.

Tipsy but still on point, Sanai remembered having thoughts of being followed. She stopped them in their tracks and scanned the area to make sure they weren't being followed or spied on.

"Why are we stopping?" her date asked, getting suspicious.

"Earlier when I pulled up, I thought I was followed here."

His feeling of suspicion turned to nervousness when he heard that. All he could think of was his wife.

"What do you mean by followed? Did you see who it was?"

"Not really sure if I was followed or not, but let's not kill the mood. If we were followed, we were followed. I want some kisses down low. Let them watch."

They crept inside the backseat and began kissing heavily. Saliva and heavy breathing were being exchanged as clothes were being taken off.

"Damn, you were naked under that dress the whole time," Sanai's date mentioned after peeling her out of the dress.

"Easy access, baby. I know what I came here for. Now give it to me," she said forcefully.

She stripped him butt naked, then started to kiss his chest and lick on his nipples. After a couple of kisses, she gradually made her way down to his manhood, which was standing at attention like a soldier in boot camp. Taking it in her mouth nice and slow, she got down to business like a hooker on a john. She even showcased her skills by not using any hands. She bobbed her head up and down, then switched to a circular motion while her date stared in amazement.

After making herself reach the highest level of horniness, she bent over and arched her back, ready for penetration. As his muscle slid in between her thighs, she let out a small moan that eventually got louder with every pelvic thrust. By this time, the windows were fogged up, and the Navigator was rocking back and forth.

"Yes! Fuck me just like that. Ooh, yes! I feel you in my stomach." Sanai continued to take the punishment with her back arched.

One by one, every stroke got her closer to climaxing. Wanting them to climax at the same time, she directed him to go deeper as she rose up and grabbed his neck while screaming out the orders. Their bodies were almost glued together. His hands were over her breasts, and his love muscle delivered infinite pleasure.

"C'mon, I want you to cum with me. Please cum with me!"

Sanai's demands got louder and louder until she couldn't scream it out no more. Her wet spot began splashing like Niagara Falls between the deep strokes as she came.

"Ooh, baby, did you cum with me?" Sanai purred.

"Yes, I did," her date answered, while trying to catch his breath.

The sexual climax was interrupted by Sanai's phone ringing. She glanced at who was calling, sent them straight to voicemail, and then continued with the conversation.

"That was so good. It even felt like we were being watched," Sanai commented while slipping back into her dress.

"You might like the sound of that, but I don't," her date replied, almost killing the moment.

"What, are you afraid it was your wife watching?" Sanai said jokingly.

"Don't joke like that. That's serious. If she were watching, you would be the first to die."

The way her date commented brought upon a strange silence. Instead of responding, Sanai just put on her shoes, gave him a kiss on the cheek, and prepared to step out the truck.

"Wait. I have a surprise for you," her date said, stopping her in her tracks.

Sanai's eyes lit up like the Fourth of July; she loved surprises.

"What is it?" she asked.

Her date reached behind the seat, grabbed a bag, and handed it to her.

"No, you didn't," Sanai said, already knowing what was inside the box.

"What? You already know what it is?"

"Yes! These are the Gucci's that I told you I wanted. Thank you." Sanai gave him a hug.

"I know just when I'm gonna rock them, too," she said, thinking about the next ladies' night out that was about to come up.

After exchanging another hug and kiss, Sanai and her date departed from each other. As she walked to her car, the craziest feeling came over her. She turned around and froze. It felt like someone was burning a hole through her back. Once the feeling passed, she hopped in her car and then circled the block to see if anybody was tailing her. After driving around twice and feeling secure that nobody was following her, she proceeded home.

Michelle

Pick Up The Pieces

Dereseé sat on the leather sofa in her office staring out the window as the April rain showered her beautiful garden and manicured lawn. She inhaled deeply, trying to breathe the pain away. She had been home for the second day without Eric, and he had not attempted to contact her at all. It was now Friday late afternoon, and she was still inside with swollen eyes. She turned to the left and caught a glimpse of the oversized photo sitting on top of the floating wall shelf.

Dereseé had been crying off and on all night, and the evidence showed on her face like a tainted crime scene. She sat awaiting the support she so desperately needed at this time. Dereseé held her cell phone in her hand as if willing it to ring and the caller being Eric. Despite her wishful thinking, Eric was still in Freakville and enjoying his last night there.

The rain stopped and the sun came out for its final showing for the night. The sixty-eight degree breeze was satisfying and still warm. Even the smell of fresh rain and the warm spring breeze blowing in through the French doors that led out to the screened patio could not cheer Dereseé up.

Dereseé rose from the sofa and made her way to the kitchen. She decided to make her and her guest some strawberry-infused Mojitos to take the edge off. As she passed the living room, she looked out of the door to see if her guest had arrived, but there was no sign of them. She continued on her journey and gathered all the necessary ingredients. Moving slowly, she began to make a big glass pitcher of her specialty Mojito as she added each ingredient.

"Damn, I'm gonna be drunk early at this rate," she said aloud.

Dereseé could hear her cell phone alerting her of a text message. She poured herself a glass and headed in the direction of her office. By the time she got there, the phone stopped ringing. As she turned the corner to enter the office, she heard her patio door open. There stood Michelle still in her scrubs. Dereseé almost dropped her drink as she held her hand over her chest.

"Girl, you scared the shit out of me."

Michelle looked at her briefly and could tell she had been crying for a long period of time.

"What's happening? You sounded crazy on the phone, and you've been crying. Talk to me, Dee."

The sound of her friend's voice and her presence made the floodgates give way. Michelle could not understand anything that she uttered.

"Okay, Dee, you're scaring me. Take a couple deep breaths and wait to speak. Where is the rest of this drink? I think I'm gonna need a few of these."

Dereseé pointed her to the kitchen as she sat and attempted to get her emotions together. After removing her shoes, Michelle headed to the kitchen, where she found a large pitcher of Mojito. She decided to grab it and some snacks before heading back to the office. When she returned, Michelle found a now calm Dereseé seated on the patio watching the sun leave footprints in the sky.

"Girl, are you okay? I was worried about you from your brief message a couple of days ago to your frantic call this afternoon."

Dereseé took a deep breath and poured another glass of strawberry-infused Mojito.

"To answer your question, no, I am not okay. I cannot believe this is my life right now. Let me start from the beginning."

Dereseé began to pour all of the events of the past three days on Michelle. The pair laughed, then cried and continued well into the night with their session. Michelle let Dereseé talk as she listened. She could not believe how insensitive Eric was with the whole swinger thing. She was more intrigued to know what Eric was doing still at the retreat while his wife was at home a hot mess.

Thinking that the emotional torture was over, Michelle took a long sigh, but Dereseé sat on the edge of her seat and gave Michelle a serious look.

"Michelle, I have more to tell you."

Michelle was exhausted with the information she had already received.

"Why are you looking like that, Dee?" Michelle responded. "This must be serious."

Desereé took a sip of her fourth Mojito. "Remember I told you that I had to get a ride from the place when I couldn't get you on the phone? Well, Chance came to pick me up."

Michelle almost choked on her drink. "What Chance? Please tell me that you're not referring to fine-ass Chance that was your former paralegal and in love with you! This story keeps getting crazier."

Desereé grabbed the pitcher from the side-table positioned in between the two comfy chairs on the patio and poured the last of the Mojito in Michelle's glass. Michelle sat back and placed her feet on the footstool.

"This is worse than I thought. How the hell did Chance and you reconnect?"

Desereé put her finger over her lips to encourage Michelle to be quiet. "Chance called me while I was in need and broken just to tell me that he wanted to speak to me about something. I got him to agree to come get me, and when he did, I was not prepared for what he wanted to tell me."

Desereé played with her cell phone as she continued. "He showed up looking scrumptious…good enough to eat! He went on and on about how he wasn't going to give up on me because we were meant to be together."

Holding up her right hand, Michelle stopped her. "Wait, wait. You're telling me that Chance drove all the way out there to give you the 'we are meant for each other' speech? He had to want something else."

Dereseé sat on the edge of her seat and looked Michelle in her eyes. "You're so right. He not only practically asked for my hand in marriage, he told me that he had proof why he knew we needed to be together. He went on to say he knew things about Eric that proves he doesn't deserve me. I immediately got defensive, Michelle. I knew Eric changed in the past few months, but I refused to confront it."

Now standing, Dereseé looked off into space while rubbing her head in despair. "To make it worse, I attacked Chance and shut him down before he could tell me what he was referring to exactly. Deep down, I didn't want to know."

Michelle just sat there with her mouth hanging open, not saying a word.

Dereseé yelled, "Say something, would you?"

Michelle's mind raced as she tried to make sense of what she was just told. "Dee, I cannot believe that bastard. What is he thinking? What could he be hiding?"

Dereseé began sobbing again. "Now Chance won't accept my calls at home or at his office."

Michelle stood with Dereseé and tried to console her as she held her in her arms. "Chance is the least of your worries right now. The question is, what does he have on Eric?"

There was no answer offered. Dereseé had cried enough in two days than she ever did in her life. The pair walked side-by-side heading into the house, as the warm air had turned into chilly night air and their emotional visit was coming to an end. As the two ladies entered the living room and headed to the kitchen, there Eric stood in the center of the room. His luggage remained at the front door.

"Ohhhh, you scared me, Eric," Dereseé yelled. "How long have you been home? I wasn't expecting you until tomorrow."

Eric looked suspicious and out of place. "I've been here for a few minutes. I decided to cut my trip short."

Michelle looked him and then her watch that read eleven o'clock. She gave him a dry hello before announcing her departure. "Well, I was just leaving. Dee, I will get with you tomorrow."

Michelle looked at Eric good. He had the same look of her clients once they were done— the look of shame. He was definitely coming from a late-night encounter, and there was nothing she could do about it.

$\mathcal{L}$ayla

Desire Within

Sanai sat at her desk singing her favorite oldie Prince song, "Insatiable", as she completed billing for the salon. She moved money around as needed and took care of payroll. The shop was lively and the usual gossip flew through the air. As the next song started, Sanai hummed to the beat. Her earphones and staying busy with work protected her from the gossip.

Her office was beautifully decorated with rich gold and royal blue throughout the space. One focal wall was painted in a Cheetah print, matching the colors throughout. Comfy large pillow seats hung from the ceiling and gave a fun vibe to her space. It was just like Sanai to think out of the box. That's how she was in every aspect of her life.

Layla tapped on Sanai's door hoping to get in and talk to her friend like she hadn't done in quite some time. For a little while now, things seemed to be awkward between them. Sanai did not answer the knock as her ears were occupied, so Layla entered the space. Sanai looked up as if to inquire what she wanted.

"Hey, girl, what's going on?" Layla said.

"Hey, Lay-Lay. I'm just finishing up some billing. What's up with you?"

Layla walked around the desk and took a seat. "Nothing. Just checking on you. We have a full house out there."

Sanai looked through the glass window on the door as if to confirm Layla's statement. All stations were occupied. Knowing Layla wanted something else, Sanai paused to gather her thoughts, but was unsure as to what it was she wanted.

Layla leaned in and played with Sanai's curls. Being Sanai's stylist made her feel a certain ownership of her hair. "So where were you last night? I called you a couple of times."

Sanai frowned and removed Layla's hand. "Girl, you're starting to freak me out. What's up with you?"

"Excuse me, why can't you just answer the fucking question?" Layla said, changing the tone of her voice.

Sanai rolled her neck as she frowned again, this time causing wrinkles to form on her forehead.

"First of all, we're best friends and business partners. Don't start treating me like I'm your spouse."

Layla backed up, folded her arms, and leaned, placing most of her weight on her right leg.

Reading her body language, Sanai continued, "Are you still mad about me leaving early when we had lunch?"

Layla didn't answer. She just gave Sanai a blank stare while still standing with her arms folded on her lean. Sanai rolled her eyes and smacked her teeth at her best friend, not understanding her actions and words.

"Look, Sanai, it's just that I'm used to you letting me know everything. Now I feel like we're drifting apart."

Sanai smiled at her friend's disposition about her becoming secretive. Judging off her reaction, she decided to apologize. She stood up and extended her arms, and they embraced. After releasing each other, Sanai sat back down and went into an explanation.

"You will never lose me, Layla." Pointing her index finger at herself and then Layla, she continued, "You and I made a pact to always stay true to each other from personal to business. Believe me, when it's time to tell you, I will. Now let's change the subject. How's my little writer's book coming along?" Sanai asked, getting excited to know about the book.

Sanai's question changed the tone of the conversation. Layla smiled; she liked to discuss the book with Sanai since it was loosely based on their lives.

"I'm almost finished. I will let you know when it's complete."

"If you weren't so worried about the who, when, and where concerning me, you would be done," Sanai said with sincerity.

Layla flagged her and sucked her teeth. She then went into her purse, pulled out her diary, sat down on the couch inside the office, and began writing. Having always seen her writing inside this book, Sanai got up and walked over to try and take it from her. Layla looked up before Sanai could reach for it and clutched it to her chest.

"You can't read this until the book is complete."

Ca`lab

Sanai shook her head, but still was anxious to read her best friend's first novel titled *B.F.F. (Best Friends Forever)*. "You screaming on me for being secretive, but you can't even show me your little diary."

*****

After typing the words *The End* in bold capital letters, Layla smiled and sighed with relief that her first manuscript was complete. She saved it and then closed her laptop right before her husband, Darren, stepped out the bathroom. Steam from the hot shower flowed inside the bedroom as he entered the bedroom with a green towel wrapped around his waist and beads of water streaming down his muscular chest. He walked over and kissed Layla on her forehead.

"It's done," Layla told him with a smile.

"Good. Now you can attend to me," Darren replied, while removing the towel and showing his soldier standing at attention.

Layla gazed at his stiffness and then saluted, knowing he was ready to invade her moistness.

"After I get out the shower, you and your little soldier can go to war," Layla said as she rose and took off her knee-length t-shirt and black lace panties.

At the sight of her naked body, he moaned and was left waiting patiently in anticipation of a great nightcap. At the sound of the water turning on, he glanced over to his left and spotted her diary on top of her laptop. Temptation burned in his gut as he warred with his curiosity. Giving in to temptation, Darren

84

hurried to grab the diary before Layla came back from her shower. He turned on the night lamp on his side of the bed, sat up, and proceeded to read.

Ten minutes later, Layla opened the bathroom door, letting out a steam cloud. For the first time in months, she actually anticipated a sexual encounter from her husband instead of using her hand and thoughts to make her climax. She walked out only for her anticipation to be buried at the sight of her husband reading her diary. Layla quickly ran to the bedside to grab the book out of his hand. He stopped her in her tracks with his right hand and held the book in the air with his left.

"So this is why I'm slowly losing my wife? I don't even recognize the person who wrote this crazy shit," Darren yelled, as the sexual tension they had orchestrated died within seconds.

"I don't know what you're talking about. Just give me my book!" Layla said, attempting to grab the book out of his masculine grip.

"You know what the fuck I'm talking about. I've been reading it for the last ten minutes. So, just know as I hold this in my left hand, you got some explaining to do."

"No, I don't. It's only notes for my book. Now give it back!"

"It sure doesn't read like notes. It reads like your words, like a diary. You're not getting this book back until I feel I've received at least a morsel of truth from you."

"What are you talking about?" Layla asked with a slight smirk.

"Bitch, don't play stupid," Darren said, wiping the schoolgirl smirk off her face.

His words felt like one hundred needles piercing her skin at the same time. He never called Layla such fowl names unless they were role-playing during foreplay. This time, she knew he meant it. As she thought about how to answer Darren's questions, his right hand that was holding her back started moving towards her neck. She remained silent. His frustration grew and pushed him over the edge. He slammed her down on the bed on her back. Layla began to kick, scream, and squirm—doing everything she could think of to escape his grasp.

"Bitch, you're lucky we have a daughter. I could choke the life out of you right now," Darren growled between clenched teeth.

Darren's rant summoned company. London came right on time. Having heard the commotion, she began knocking on the door.

"Mommy! Mommy!" London yelled as she knocked.

Darren threw the book across the room, hitting a lamp and causing it to shatter on the floor. This startled London, who was standing on the outside of the bedroom. Not knowing what was taking place, she started to scream and cry. Darren finally let go and stomped over to his closet where he began shuffling through some clothes. Layla lay crying on her back, devastated from her husband's actions. Fully dressed in a Nike jogging suit, he stood over her and addressed her again.

"Attend to our daughter. You can at least do that! Or is that not scandalous enough for you?"

Layla rose to run over and open the door, instantly consoling London.

"London, stop crying, baby. Everything is okay. Now go back to your room."

"But, Mommy..." London began to say until she was cut off.

"No buts right now. Go back to bed," Layla said with tears still streaming down her face.

As London ran back into her room, Layla rose from her knees to see her husband putting on his Air Maxes and then grabbing his keys.

"And where are you going? We're not finished."

Darren didn't respond. He just stared at her with a look that could have killed her a thousand times.

After a brief second of staring at each other in silence, he replied, "You're not in the position to ask me anything. Just know I'm leaving because I need some time to breathe."

Layla tried to stop him from leaving, but he overpowered her, tossing her back on the bed. Once she heard the front door slam, she felt like she lost her husband forever and began to cry helplessly. The anticipation and excitement from her manuscript being completed had disappeared maybe forever. A broken Layla walked slowly to her closet and secured her diary in its rightful place.

Michelle

Hide and Seek

Michelle walked briskly to make it to her destination. Several days had passed since her emotional rollercoaster with Desereé, and she was in pursuit of some answers. Michelle had a theory but struggled to put the pieces together. She only had a brief time in between work and meeting with a john to find Chance's office and get some of the answers she sought.

Michelle was not comfortable traveling the streets with her bag full of tricks, but it was Wednesday and her day to ride public transportation to work and then to her standing appointment after work. A high-profile client with a lot to loose, her john did not like any attention or traceable items, such as license plates, being visible. In addition, they met at a different location weekly.

Michelle scanned the office buildings looking for the address of his firm as it was listed on Google. She stopped to ask a street vendor where the office of Chance Levick could be found.

Chuckling, the vendor said, "He needs to pay me a fee for GPS service. People ask me about that office a few times a day. A gentleman just asked me for the office address about an hour ago." The vendor continued as he scratched his head. "You're about five offices from your destination. Cross the street and enter those large double doors in the center of the block. The office list and names are located in the lobby. Good luck. Don't forget to stop back to get your fresh fruit salad before you leave."

Michelle waved at the man and flashed her sexy smile. "Thanks, sir."

She continued on her journey, counting the building doors along her way. She finally arrived at the fifth building. The lobby was bustling with people going the opposite way than Michelle. With it being 5:30 p.m., it was a long shot that he was even still at his office.

Chance office was on the 8th floor. Michelle entered the elevator and pressed the number eight. She wondered what she would run into when she got to his office. Would he even be willing to speak to her about Eric? The bling sound alerted her that she had reached her destination. She exited the elevator and headed toward his suite. The pretty green letters on the glass door listed the associates' names and hours of operation. The office closed at four o'clock Monday through Friday.

"Awww, shit. This trip was for nothing." Michelle let out a loud sigh.

She could see a light on inside of the office. She also could see someone sitting at the desk. Desperate for answers, Michelle knocked and called the number on the door. The shadow did not move or change positions. Thinking that was rude for the person to ignore her, she increased her force on the door, knocking harder. The glass door opened a few inches as the door was not secured. She walked in slowly while yelling for someone.

"Hello? Chance? Anyone?"

A voice in the distance replied, "I'm sorry, we're closed!"

In a polite, timid, high-pitched voice, which was a total change from her normal, mid-range, authoritative tone, Michelle yelled back, "Excuse me, I'm so sorry to bother you, but I need to speak with Chance Levick. It's urgent."

A brief commotion erupted from the back office. Suddenly, a tall, statuesque man appeared with a very annoyed look on his face. When he fixed his eyes upon the image standing before him, his look softened.

"How are you, Michelle?" Chance's words flowed from his lips in a smooth baritone sound that sent vibrations up and down Michelle's spine.

She smiled, enjoying the warmth that brewed between her legs.

Chance walked toward Michelle. "What are you doing here?"

His piercing hazel eyes struck Michelle. They looked so beautiful against his dark chocolate skin, very exotic.

When she realized she was staring, she finally replied, "I had to see you…to speak to you about a very important matter. I don't have much time, though, because I'm working."

Chance smiled, flashing his perfect teeth. "Still the same, Michelle…all business. At least tell me how you've been."

"I'm fine. How about yourself?"

Chance walked toward his office as he interacted in Michelle's small talk. "I'm making it. Still trying to make my mark in the industry and steal your girlfriend's heart."

He chuckled as the words escaped his lips. Michelle was fond of Chance but didn't have time for his long drawn-out stories.

Chance and Micki met a few months before he started working as Eric's paralegal. After their first sexual encounter, Chance became one of her favorite clients. They had a strong attraction toward one another, but he knew their relationship was strictly business. When he saw Dereseé his first day on the job, he was convinced she was his soul mate and planned to win her love at any cost. He made his intentions clear to Dereseé and anyone else who would listen. Dereseé shared Chance's constant plays for her with Michelle, who could not risk exposing her dark side to her best friend nor could she break her heart. Michelle and Chance had not seen each other for business since he fell for Dereseé. Micki looked at Chance with hunger in her eyes. Business or not, he was a great lay. She forced herself to get back to business.

"Look, Chance, I can't act like this is a social call. I'm here for some information."

Chance's expression turned serious. "What type of information?"

Michelle continued, "Dereseé told me that you and she met the other day, and you had some information about Eric."

Chance frowned. "Yes, we did, but did she also tell you that she shut me down when I attempted to tell her about that low-down dirty dog?"

Michelle leaned against his broad desk while he shuffled papers around on his desk. "Yes, she did tell me how harsh she was on you."

Placing his work in a neat pile, Chance asked, "What do you have to do with Eric?"

"I have some information I'm trying to confirm, and if your info matches mine, then I have an obligation to protect my friend."

Standing, Chance walked toward his file cabinet, took out an envelope, and tossed it on the desk.

"This is what I have compiled on Mr. Eric for the past few months up until a couple of days ago."

Michelle approached the envelope with caution. She almost was too afraid to find out what the contents were inside. When Michelle opened the package, staring back at her were piles of papers that had what looked like transcripts of conversations. Chance leaned in to look over her shoulder as if it was his first time seeing the material. Michelle continued to view the papers.

Chance's cell phone rang once, then again and stopped. He continued to discuss the crazy text messages Eric was sending and receiving. His phone rang again. This time, he made it to the phone in time.

"Hello. Chance Levick speaking."

Chance became silent and listened to the caller. He was startled when his crystal gavel went crashing to the floor along with the envelope and pictures Michelle had discovered.

Michelle fell back on the white leather sofa across from Chance's desk. Startled, Chance ended his call and ran to console Michelle. She sat quietly for a moment as Chance began picking up the contents of envelope.

"Look, I have to go. I just got an important call, and I have to meet someone quickly."

"No! No! NOOOOO!" Michelle yelled to the top of her lungs. "Those pictures are horrible. Why? Why?"

Chance attempted to calm her down. He knew what Eric was doing was bad, but he couldn't believe how hard Michelle was taking it. Tears streamed down her face as she stared in the face of a possible death sentence. Chance gathered all he needed for his spontaneous meeting and helped Michelle to the door.

Stopping at the door, she looked into his eyes and sternly said, "Chance, I need that file!"

Chance returned her gaze. "Now what makes you think I will do that? The contents of this file is my only chance of getting Dereseé to leave that fool and finally be with someone who knows how to treat her right. Besides, what stake do you have in this information anyway?"

A mix of anger and desperation fell over Michelle's voice. "Look, Chance, I don't have time to explain now, but you have to trust me on this."

Chance trusted no one. The last time he did, it backfired, causing him to lose the one woman he loved. There was no way he would allow someone he paid to have sex with in the past to just walk away with the one thing that could bring Dereseé back to him.

"Look, Michelle, I don't know what's going on, but if you think you're going to come in here, flash a sexy smile, bat your eyelashes, and walk out of here with my information, then you are surely mistaken."

Chance headed over to the file cabinet to put the file back in its proper place, when Michelle stepped in front of him.

"What the hell are you doing?" he asked.

"Look, I told you. I need that file! If you would stop acting so self-absorbed, you would realize this goes way beyond you," she spat.

Chance grew annoyed. "Get out of my way, Michelle. I don't have time for your bullshit. Now, I've already told you that I have a meeting."

Michelle refused to move. Growing angry, Chance pushed past Michelle with a force that sent her stumbling backwards into the open file cabinet drawer. In a fit of rage, Michelle retaliated by throwing her entire body into him, knocking him off balance.

"You crazy bitch!" Chance yelled.

One hand reached out and connected with Michelle's throat while the other desperately held on to the file. The two were locked in a heated struggle, dancing around like a couple on *Dancing with the Stars* whose routine had gone terribly wrong, and all over the contents of the file. That, in addition to what Michelle knew would not only ruin Eric's life but Deseree's, as well. Michelle was determined to do whatever she could to pry that file out of Chance's hands. At that moment, all she wanted was to break free from his grasp and get to her bag of tricks to retrieve one of her syringes which contained a cocktail that would knock him out permanently.

Chance's hand was still clamped tightly around her neck. Michelle began feeling lightheaded. Images of Dereseé's face played like a movie in her head. All she could think about was what this would do to her. Then, she realized that leaving Chance's office without the file was not an option. She had to fight for her life and her friend.

In the midst of their struggle, Michelle was able to turn Chance around so his back was now facing the open file cabinet drawer. Suddenly, her adrenaline went into fight mode. Michelle pushed Chance into the cabinet, causing him to loosen his grip on her neck. She repeated this at least three more times until he fell to the floor. When Chance fell, he hit his head on the base of his chair and passed out cold.

Michelle called out to Chance several times, but there was no response. Anxiety-ridden, Michelle quickly retrieved her medical bag and checked him to make sure he was still breathing. She then dragged Chance to the couch and proceeded to clean up any evidence of her ever being in Chance's office.

After gathering the file with the incriminating evidence against Eric, she shoved it into her medical bag. She regained her composure, picked up all her belongings, and headed for the door while trying to contemplate her next move.

Sanai

Dirty laundry

"Stop...please...wait."

Her whispers of desperation went unnoticed. Sanai grasped at the air trying to gain control of her body. She could see the ceiling of her bedroom, but it appeared blurry and distorted. The smell of jasmine in the air kept her senses working. She could hear the flicker of her scented candle on the nightstand. Sanai's body quivered from pain and pleasure. The sexy hands around her neck had turned into a dangerous trap. She mustered up enough strength to thrust her lower body upward and break free of her lover's grip, sending her playmate plummeting to the floor.

"Damn, dude. What, you trying to kill me? I was about to be green. I'm not trying to die just so you can bust your nut."

The pair broke out in laughter as she held her throat. Sanai had summoned a male suitor to give her some good afternoon sex before she completed her day. She never brought men home to her comfort zone, but he was different, and the fact that he was spoken for and couldn't spend many nights out made things a little harder.

"You got me sprung, babe. I'm so charged that it's all I can think about. I'm sorry I got carried away, but you send me to new heights."

Sanai sat up on the side of her king-size bed still rubbing her neck. "Awww, you make me smile, but we both know we can never be anything but what we are. So what are we doing?"

Just as the two were getting ready to have a long overdue talk, Sanai's phone rang at the highest volume, interrupting their flow. She got up to retrieve her headset and was startled when she saw the number. The caller ID read Law Office. Sanai reluctantly answered.

"Hello."

There was a pause before a female's voice said, "Hello, Sanai?" The words were posed more as a question than a salutation.

Sanai cleared her throat. "Yes. Who's calling?"

There was silence and then sniffles.

"Hello, Sanai. It's Deseree. I'm calling to cancel our mall run. Something came up and I have to handle it."

Sanai cleared her throat again before speaking. "Okay. What's wrong, girl? You sound shaky. Is everything okay?" Sanai asked in a concerned tone.

"I'm okay. I just have something to handle. I'll see you tomorrow."

Sanai felt bad down in the pit of her stomach. She could tell Deseree was different on the phone and seemed to be upset. She hated secrets; she knew what they did to relationships and what they made people do even though she coveted some secrets of her own. Sanai turned to continue entertaining her guest, but he had let himself out while she was chatting with her friend. She scanned her bathroom and headed down the steps to the kitchen where she found a note.

Thanks for the fun, babe. I had to go. I have a few meetings. Will call you later. Sorry for running out, but I didn't want to disturb your call.
XOXO

Sanai crumpled up the note in her right hand, sucked her teeth, then looked up toward the ceiling and said, "I'm sure you're sorry."

She didn't like how she felt about his abrupt disappearance. Sanai knew she would have to end their fun soon before things got ugly.

Sanai made her way to the refrigerator and grabbed a Greek yogurt. Then she sat at her kitchen table and stared out of the window as she watched the sunlight flicker off the bay window. She began thinking back to what started her on the path she was on. The downward spiral with men just seemed to get worse once her relationship ended with King due to his early demise.

Sanai, now full grown, was still stuck in the past. Her stagnation reminded her of what a terrible person she was day after day. She started using sex to ease the pain years ago, telling herself that she was in control of her destiny and not able to be hurt this way. When, in actuality, she was far worse than she let on. The core of who she claimed to be hinged on loyalty to those that was in her circle. She had gotten so used to blurring the lines of boundaries until no line even existed at this point. She was involved in things she always swore she would never do, and it was overwhelming her. Tears began to well in her eyes and then stream down her face as she remembered what love once felt like and then what it felt like to lose it.

As she stared off into space, the thing that haunted her daily, but which she never voiced to anyone else, came back to her in living color.

Sanai rushed home to get ready to go see her favorite man. She was so in love with King, and he swore he was head over heels for her. Everybody in the neighborhood and those that encountered the pair in passing knew they were a match made in heaven. Sanai was always the down-for-whatever type when it came to her man, and she liked to keep things spicy.

It was a spring day and just a few days away from her and King's 3rd anniversary. She planned on surprising him with a quick pop up. Sanai hurried to her room to prepare for her romantic assembly. She had it all planned for weeks and was ready to give King a time he would never forget. She gathered all of her freaky props, her beautiful card and gift for him, and then headed to his condo.

She pulled up and was happy to see he was home. King was very successful at what he did and had money, so he always kept his moves unpredictable. Sanai knew the only way to surprise him would be to get him before their actual anniversary and at a time when he expected her to be at work.

Sanai was dressed to impress. She adorned her beautiful frame with a strapless sundress that exposed all of her dangerous curves. Underneath her dress she wore nothing but a neatly trimmed wet-box. Her sexy legs were the stars of the show in her four-inch strappy sandals. Lip-gloss hugged her full lips as she prepared them for kisses. She was ready to do things to King that was illegal in some states. She was a generous lover, especially since he would be her husband someday.

Sanai walked toward his front door and practiced her stance for when he opened up to see her. King's condo was on the first floor and boasted luxury with a picture-perfect garden view.

Sanai quickly went around the side of the building to hide some of her gifts, like the big teddy bear she had purchased for him. She quickly made it back to his front door, now on the top step and ready to surprise him. She tapped on the door and then rang the bell. She could hear the music on throughout the space and was unsure what room King was in. Since his condo was spacious, sometimes it took him a while to hear someone at the door. So, Sanai decided to call his cell phone and announce her presence. The phone rang a few times but there was no answer.

Now worried that something was wrong, Sanai walked back around the side of the house. The window to his suite bathroom was the only window on the side of the building besides the sliding doors that led to a small patio off of his bedroom. She made up her mind and was preparing to climb on the patio, if necessary. For privacy reasons, the bathroom window was too high to see anything, which made it hard to find out what was going on inside of King's place. Sanai began to get frustrated and worried even more because his main car was in the parking lot, but there was no movement in response to her calls and door knocking. She leaned against the wall under the bathroom window gathering her thoughts.

Sanai listened closely and could now hear water running. She was relieved knowing he was probably in the shower. She began to gather her gifts so she could wait out his long shower in her car. As she bent down to pick up the last hidden gift, she heard muffled sounds of two voices and what sounded like smacks. The sounds got louder as a female's voice screamed out in pleasure. She froze as the music stopped and the screams became louder. Sanai fell to her knees. The shower water cut off and now a muffled conversation could be heard. The words would haunt her forever.

"Silky, pass me my towel from behind the door."

Sanai wanted to vomit. Silky, her first cousin on her dad's side and known slut, was with her man. In shock and still not wanting to believe King would betray her this way, she dialed his number again, hoping the voice she heard in the bathroom was not his. This time, it rang once and went straight to voicemail.

She sobbed hysterically. Her world shattered as she attempted to pick up the pieces of betrayal. She quickly ran to her car and vanished as if she were never there.

Sanai could not breathe. Hyperventilating, she gasped for air as she drove. The feeling of betrayal felt too much like the day her mother chose drugs over her family, leaving her to be raised by her father and his ghetto people. She had to make King pay; he had been her refuge for so long. In an instant, he became the eye of the storm as he ripped her soul out and stepped on it. Once home, she paced the floor screaming and crying. Her body literally ached from the emotional pain. She had witnessed the story of her and King die right before her eyes.

After about a few hours of mourning her relationship, she scrolled through her phone and came across fine-ass Corey's number. She had always said she was reserving his number as a backup plan if King ever messed up. She wiped her eyes and dialed his number slowly. The phone rang once and he picked up.

"Yo, baby, talk to me."

Corey was smooth like that and powerful, too. He and King were direct rivals on the street and each other's competition. Corey had been trying to secure Sanai for years, even before King. He was admittedly obsessed with her since high school.

"Hey, Corey. What you getting into today?"

Corey paused and laughed. *"Whatever you want to get into, sweetheart. The question is will your man mind what we're about to get into?"*

Sanai hated that he was insecure when it came to King. That was one reason she never really took him seriously.

"I'm calling you, so that's all that matters. Come scoop me up in about twenty minutes."

"Enough said, lil' momma. I'll see you in twenty minutes."

"Cool. I'll be outside."

Sanai quickly prepared for her revenge date. She was not sure what she was going to do, but she knew her and King were over. For him to screw another chic in the condo where they share moments was lowdown, but right before their anniversary was downright disgusting and unforgivable.

Just like clockwork, Corey arrived in twenty minutes, pulling up in his cream-colored Escalade that shined like new money. Sanai struck a pose, and he whistled at her in a flirtatious way.

"Hop on in, lil' momma."

She did just that and directed him to the expressway. He took her directions with full trust. About thirty minutes later, they arrived at Brandywine Creek, where the warm weather and bubbling water made for a picture-perfect day. Corey pulled up to the edge of the creek and parked. He glanced over at Sanai, and she gave him her award-winning fake smile.

"So what's been up with you, Sanai? I see you looking good!"

Sanai was hurting and had no time for memory lane; she just wanted to feel better.

As she grabbed his right hand and put it up her dress where a nice surprise greeted him, she replied, *"Nothing's really been up. Just thinking 'bout you. Now, do you want all this wet sugar or did you come to talk about your feelings?"*

Corey's crotch gave her the answer she wanted. Sanai unzipped his shorts and was happy to see his package. "Mmmmm," she moaned as she took him in her hand. His manhood was so hard that the tip was almost as big as the shaft.

The pair kissed like they were in love. It was at that moment when she realized sex could take her pain away for a brief moment. Sanai kissed and bit his earlobes and neck as he squirmed and moaned.

"I knew you were a good lover by the way you walk," Corey said, sprung over the foreplay.

Sanai placed her right index finger over Corey's lips, encouraging him to be silent while she mounted him and slid down on his rod extremely slow. The wetness ran down his love muscle as she sat completely down until their pelvis touched.

"Mmmm, Corey, this is nice. So hard and big just for me."

Sanai went up, down, and circular until she climaxed over and over. Corey didn't want the moment to end. So, he gritted his teeth and used all of his might not to climax too soon. Sanai could tell he was holding back. The power she felt on top of him was addictive. She was powerful again, not crying and hurting. Sanai grabbed the back of Corey's neck and stared him deep in his eyes. On the verge of the biggest orgasm she had ever experienced, she began talking to him in a sensual voice while staring at him.

"Corey, I'm about to explode and it's all because of you. Mmmm…what would you do to keep me here? Tell me now."

Corey's body started to shake uncontrollably. "Oh shit, Sanai."

She rode him harder and commanded that he answer her.

"Come on, Corey. We gonna explode together. Now focus, baby. What would you do to keep me making you feel like this?"

Corey's hips moved faster and faster as he yelled, "Anything, Si, anything! Oh shit…oh shit. I'm blasting…oooooooo!"

Sanai hopped off of him and grabbed the base of his rod to slow the orgasm.

"Oh my God, girl, what are you doing?" Corey asked in a weak voice.

Sanai played with him, giving him mixed feelings of pleasure. "Okay, baby, this is it. When I let go, you're going to squirt everywhere."

Sanai removed her hand and pressed the line between the scrotum and anus with her thumb as she fell face first in his lap, taking all of him inside of her mouth. Corey climbed backward up the seat while screaming to the top of his lungs.

When Sanai realized she had him, she looked up in his face between slurps and moaned, "Would you kill for me?"

In a state of euphoria he had never experienced before, Corey shouted, "Yes, baby, I would killll for you!"

Sanai wiped her mouth and Corey panted to catch his breath, not knowing he had just sold his soul to the devil. She laid the seat back and gazed out of the window, enjoying the feeling she had just experienced. She never wanted to come down off of the high.

Sanai did not even feel the tears pouring out of her eyes until her cell phone ringing interrupted her daydream. She checked the caller ID, and it was Layla calling. She cried even harder as she sent her straight to voicemail. Her new fling had her tripping and wanting to feel a real connection with someone again.

Michelle

Game Face

Eric walked quickly with strides of precision. He had to hurry to get to his destination. Thoughts raced through his mind about the conversation he had walked in on between Michelle and Dereseé. He could not believe Chance was still in play for his wife. Eric was arrogant and thought his shit didn't stink. Therefore, his infidelity was a moot point. He was sure he possessed Dereseé, and he wanted nothing else but to make Chance pay for what he was trying to do.

Eric stopped at a small coffee shop downtown and purchased an extra strong cup of espresso. He smiled as he entered the area. It was a nostalgic vibe as he remembered the first time he had a steamy hot cup of joe from the busy place. Trevor had introduced him to the place on one of his late-night case studies, and he couldn't stop smiling about how Trevor paid close attention to detail and knew exactly what he liked after just one time of ordering for him.

Eric gathered his beverage from the young redhead and paid her an extra five dollars for being so polite. He continued his strides and his thoughts.

"What could Chance possibly have to talk to Dereseé about me?" he whispered to himself. "I have not seen him or talked to him in years. This shit has got to end tonight."

Eric checked his watch to view his window of opportunity to handle his business with Chance. He had to do some digging to find out where Chance was now working, and he planned on paying him a visit.

*****

Michelle had just left Chance, and she could not get the images of Eric and Trevor out of her mind. Eric had become a down-low brother and a bonafied freak. From what Trevor reported, he was not promiscuous and had to contract it from his lover. Michelle shook her head so much while walking the streets of Philadelphia that she got a cramp in her neck.

As she approached the subway, she decided not to even bother. Michelle did something she had never done since she met her first john years ago. She pulled out her phone and cancelled her appointment for the night. Michelle was in no mood for sex, not even if she was getting five thousand dollars for the night.

She walked some more and thought about how she would confront Eric without Dereseé knowing. She wanted to get evidence before letting the cat out of the bag. She just hoped Despised Deseree stayed mad at him long enough to keep him away from her goodies. From the seriousness of his actions on their retreat, Eric probably wouldn't get any sex from Deseree for a long time.

Turning the corner of 15th and Market, Michelle hailed a cabby as he rode by. She was in no mood for public transportation and needed to get home quickly. With their girls' night quickly approaching, she had a very short time to find out answers or this may be the last Cocktale session.

Michelle arrived home and could not get out of her clothes fast enough. She dropped everything in her living room and headed upstairs with the envelope she had stolen from Chance in hand. Michelle sat in her room looking over the documents in Chance's file. Each transcript and picture with Eric and his down-low lover took her feelings on a rollercoaster ride. This was not a normal occurrence for her, and truthfully, it didn't feel good. Becoming involved with Deseree's drama had her in a quagmire. Nevertheless, she was her friend, and as her friend, she felt she had to do something.

Michelle continued to study the files, especially the pictures of Eric, Trevor, and a female whom she couldn't identify. She scanned the photos carefully to see if there were any clues that would help her make out this mystery woman. She stared at the photos to the point of frustration. The woman's face was either covered or the image was too out of focus for Michelle to make a positive identification. It was eating her alive not knowing the identity of the mystery woman. The thought of the three of them being responsible for possibly sentencing her friend to a lifetime heartache, and eventually death, cut her like a knife.

Michelle knew there was something she had to do to avenge her friend. She continued to look through the recorded transcripts of the cell phone text messages. Suddenly, something in the file jumped out at her. It was the text messages between Eric and Trevor. Michelle became nauseous at the sight of the words on the page.

Hey, babe. I'm here at the coffee house. Where are you?

Eric's words stirred rage inside of Michelle as she continued reading further.

On my way, boo. I'm walking toward the shop now. Just order something for me. You know what I like.

Yes, I know. Café Breva. I got it. Now bring yo' sexy ass on! I've gotta hurry up and get back to work. You know how Dereeé gets.

"I've got to figure out a way to get that son of a bitch! He has got to pay," Michelle said aloud.

She sat and stared at the pictures while plotting her revenge. Then, she smiled as her brain churned out what she thought was the perfect plan.

"If I have to spend the rest of my life in hell, then so be it. But, trust and believe, you'll get there before I do," Michelle mumbled to herself

*****

Dereeé arrived home much later than usual. After pulling in her well-lit driveway, she sat in the car for a few minutes. The tension between her and Eric was still evident, and she hated to argue. Although devastated by Eric's actions, she was willing to put on a brave face and play her part until she could figure out what to do.

Despreé scrutinized her reflection in the rearview mirror. Her tresses were out of place, and she appeared disheveled. She puckered her lips, reapplied her lip-gloss, and ran her fingers through her curly hair. Despreé then inhaled air into her lungs and turned the car ignition off. She could see the living room and kitchen lights were on.

Despreé exited her black Mercedes convertible and secured her prize with the flick of her car remote. Although she lived in the posh section of King of Prussia, she always aired on the side of caution. Despreé walked slowly to her front door; the warm night air felt amazing on her skin. Her hands trembled a little, and she worried about the questions Eric would have about her late arrival.

Bracing herself, Despreé opened the door with her key. She entered the house and placed her belongings down to find no sign of Eric. Walking deeper into the home, she looked in his office and in the kitchen. Finally, she opened the door to the garage to find an empty space where his car usually occupied. All that lingered was the smell of his cologne.

She headed upstairs to start her bath and retire before she had to face Eric's return.

Despreé` tossed and turned after she finally fell off to sleep. She could not get the images out of her head and the residuals of Eric's behavior lately. She rolled over and looked at the clock. The time was eleven o'clock. There still was no sign of Eric.

Dereseé picked up the phone to call him and hung up the receiver before she could go through with it. She had things heavy on her mind, so she dialed Michelle's number to ease the load. As soon as Dereseé hit the last number and heard the line ring once, Eric's footsteps could be heard approaching. Dereseé hung up and turned on the eleven o'clock news.

$\mathcal{L}ayla$

Pick Up The Pieces

It was a whole day since Layla had seen or heard from Darren. She left him several voicemails, but received no response. With a full day ahead of her, she was not happy that they were at odds. Darren was so hypocritical and controlling. He wanted to walk on the wild side and not pay the consequences.

As Layla prepared for work, she decided now was the time to present her book that she worked so hard on. An emotional wreck, Layla attempted to pull herself together. She walked over to her desk positioned in the corner of the room, picked up her finished manuscript, and tossed it in her bag before heading out.

*****

Layla sat in the office of Dennis, an editor at her job. She was excited to hear his feedback on the first four chapters of *B.F.F.* While reading, he looked up, smiled, and continued to read. He repeated these actions as he engaged in the light reading. Layla followed his actions and came to her own conclusion that he was enjoying the first part. This made her light up inside like a 100-watt light bulb. After completing the chapters, he folded his hands on his desk. After a brief silence, he spoke as Layla sat waiting in anticipation for his feedback.

"So *B.F.F.* sounds like a bestseller to me," Dennis said with a grin. "I like what I've read so far, and it seems like it's going to get more interesting. Tell you what, Layla. I'm going to get straight to the point."

Dennis rose from his chair, walked around his desk, and sat on the edge in front of Layla.

"I'm going to be your agent with this and take it to my friend who's an editor at a major company. All I would be asking for my services is ten percent."

"Wow! Thank you, Dennis. I really appreciate that." Layla stood up and gave him a hug while grinning from ear to ear. "When should I expect the call from you?" Layla asked before exiting his office.

"Give me two weeks. I'll see what he says. If you don't here from me by then, call me."

"Will do, and thank you again, Dennis."

Layla's soul illuminated from the great news she just received. She had to call someone, and the first person she thought of was Sanai. She quickly pulled out her cell phone and dialed her number.

"What's up, girl?" Sanai answered.

"Sanai, I'm about to get a deal for my book, girl!" Layla yelled into her phone, startling a couple of coworkers to the point where they closed their office doors.

"Congrats! I'm happy for you, Layla."

There was a brief pause after Sanai spoke. She then heard sniffles coming from the other end of the phone. The sniffles turned into sobbing.

"Layla, why are you crying, girl?"

"'Cause King isn't here to celebrate my accomplishment with me."

The words pierced Sanai's soul and made her feel low. Deep down inside, she knew that she was the cause of Layla's pain.

Shaking off her grimy feeling, she breathed deeply and said, "Layla, get yourself together. He's here still looking over you."

Layla began sobbing harder as she stood in the bathroom crying out her soul in front of the mirror.

"And that's not all. I'm losing my husband."

Sanai couldn't believe what she just heard. She always joked with Layla and told her the world would end the day they would get a divorce.

Sanai stood to her feet and leaned on her desk. "Wait, wait. Back up. Say that again."

Layla leaned on the cold tile wall in the women's restroom.

"I said I'm losing my husband," Layla repeated, speaking through her tears.

Sanai shook her head at the sound of Layla crying. From the sound of her over the phone, this reminded her of when she was at King's funeral.

"Layla, I'm on my way to be with you so we can talk."

"Meet me at the house. I'm on my way to pick up London."

"Okay. I'm clocking out in a couple of minutes."

*****

Sanai pulled up to Layla's house, beating her there. She knew from the sight of two cars in the driveway that Layla still wasn't there. Only Darren's navy 745 BMW along with a Jaguar XK8 were parked in front of the house. She pulled out her cell to call Layla, but then looked up to see her pulling up behind Darren's car. Layla walked over to Sanai's car as Sanai got out to meet her. As they embraced in a tight hug, Layla instantly began sobbing on her shoulder.

"C'mon, girl, get it together. You just received some good news. I'm quite sure whatever happened between you and D can be nipped in the bud. Secondly, I want to see who's driving this Jag. It better not be a bitch or we're going to jail."

Layla didn't respond. She just removed herself from Sanai's clutch to attend to London who was at the door doing the pee-pee dance.

"Mom, I got to go bad," London yelled.

After Layla opened the door, London ran upstairs, while Sanai followed Layla to the voices coming from the kitchen. Upon entering, they found Darren sitting at the table with a Caucasian male dressed in a dapper black stripe suit. Sanai spoke to Darren, but didn't receive a response back. Unfamiliar with the man sitting in her kitchen, Layla began to express her frustration.

"What's going on here, and who's this man in my kitchen? I haven't seen you in a whole day. Where were you?"

The man that accompanied Darren turned red, and Darren threw his hands in the air.

Fed up with the tension between him and Layla, he yelled back, "Really? You want to talk now? Is that what you really want?"

Sanai could tell things were getting heated and didn't want any part of their conversation. Furthermore, she did not understand why Darren was throwing her shady looks and not speaking to her. Before the real fireworks could start, Sanai butted in.

"I know this isn't the perfect time to be asking, Layla, but can I borrow those red bottoms I love so much for girls' night out," she asked, projecting her voice as she retreated out of the kitchen.

"With pleasure," Layla replied, then turned back to Darren and his guest with her lips poked out and arms folded across her chest, waiting for an explanation.

Darren gave her a disgusting glare while also folding his arms and letting out some steam. The gentleman spoke as a tension cloud formed above them all.

"Look, Darren, I'll give you some time to think this move through. Give me a call when you're ready," he said, rising and grabbing his suitcase.

As he walked past Layla to exit the kitchen, he extended his hand and introduced himself.

"Hello, I'm Attorney Michael Dougherty of Dougherty and Dougherty."

"I don't care who you are. Just get the fuck out so I can talk to my husband."

Michael headed for the door promptly. After hearing the front door close, Layla turned back around to face Darren, who was still stuck with the same face of death.

"A lawyer? Are you serious?"

"Look, you're leaving me no choice. I don't even know who I'm married to at this point," Darren said. Then he got up and walked over to the sink, his back facing Layla as she stared out of the window.

"What do you mean, Darren?" Layla said, tears forming in her eyes.

"Don't start that bullshit crying routine, because it's not going to work." Darren turned around and leaned his rear against the sink.

As he finished speaking, London ran downstairs for an after-school snack but was stopped in her tracks.

"Ooh, baby, go back upstairs. Your father and I are having a conversation."

At the top of the stairs, Sanai called out for London.

"London! Come upstairs with Auntie Sanai."

London followed the commands of Sanai, who was heading to retrieve the shoes she asked to borrow.

Once London went back up the stairs, the pair continued.

"So are you going to tell me now?" Darren asked.

"Tell you what, Darren?" Layla said, raising her voice out of frustration.

"Do you want to be married to me? 'Cause for the past six months, you've changed, and it's bugging me the fuck out."

Layla stood with her back against the wall and her arms folded, trying not to show any guilt while answering his question truthfully.

Upstairs, Sanai went back and forth from the bedroom to the top of the steps, being nosy and trying to get the scoop. She decided to grab the shoes and leave since she knew Layla would call and give her an ear full anyway. Once inside the closet, she spotted the shoebox and opened it to gaze at the pair of shoes she always envied Layla for having before her. Sanai then poked around Layla's closet for more items to borrow before proceeding downstairs. Ready to leave, she wasn't going to wait until they finished arguing. So, she headed towards the kitchen and poked her head in.

"Sorry to interrupt, but I'm out girl."

Layla turned to face her with her arms stretched. "Okay. Give me a hug."

The two embraced in a sisterly hug. After letting go, Layla noticed Sanai wasn't carrying a shoebox and figured she had changed her mind about wearing them.

"I'll call you later," Layla said before Sanai exited. Then she walked over and sat down at the kitchen table. "Look, Darren—"

Darren stopped her in mid-sentence. "No, I don't wanna hear it. You listen to me. I want my wife back, and she better return quick, fast, and in a hurry. Or…"

"Or else what?" Layla yelled, banging her hands on the table.

"Or else I'm leaving," he threatened.

Layla didn't know how to feel. This moment was bittersweet for her. She had just received the great news that her book might get published, and then she came home to find out her husband was considering a divorce.

"You would really leave me and London?"

"If it came down to it, yes, I would."

"You know what, Darren? Get the fuck out so I can think!" Layla yelled.

Darren took a deep breath and walked past Layla, grabbing his keys off the table and heading for the door. Before leaving, he left her with some final words.

"The choice is up to you. I laid everything out on the table. Now the ball is in your court."

Layla didn't respond. She just put her hand up, signaling for him to leave her presence. She needed time to think about the next chapter in her life.

Divas' Night Out-Great Expectations

Dereseé awoke with a headache. She placed one foot at a time on the floor as she prepared her body for the day. She wished she had taken the day off because she wanted to get ready for the night out with her friend, but work came first.

She reached over to her nightstand where the Motrin had sat for the past week or more. Then she turned the television on and headed to the on-suite bathroom to procure some water to take her pills. She could not get what Chance last said about Eric out of her mind. She still didn't know how she would confront Eric to find out what was going on. It just didn't make any sense, and she knew the firm could not survive a scandal this big. While excited to hang out with her girls, Desereé was perplexed by her quandary. She solved problems on a daily basis at work, but could not seem to shake the whirlwind of problems her life had been during the past week.

Dereseé swallowed her pain medication and headed downstairs to locate Eric. She practiced what to say to him in her head, but first, she would assess his mood. He was sure to be reactive to their conversation if he was not grounded and happy. She descended the large staircase while calling his name.

"Eric, where are you, babe?"

She had not called him babe since the week prior…before all of the problems started.

She received no answer. Dereseé approached the kitchen with caution, hoping he was in the breakfast nook with the news on. As she turned the corner, she found a cold empty kitchen with no Eric in sight. With squinted eyes and while holding her forehead, she searched the room for the time. She located the clock; the time read 11:30 a.m.

Dereseé had slept in later than she would have liked.

Approaching the island, Dereseé spotted a note from Eric. She read the contents and just shook her head. Eric explained to her that he was going to the office early and then off to meet with clients for lunch.

Dereseé proceeded to prepare a late afternoon brunch and make moves for divas' night out. She would have to work a half-day in order to catch up on the big case she's working on.

*****

Layla entered her house carrying bags from Nordstrom to ready herself for ladies' night. She wasn't going to let the events that took place with her husband stop her from having fun with her friend, but the thought of having to mend their issues lingered within her brain.

She went straight upstairs to their room, only to walk in and see Darren lying on his back with his arms behind his head and watching television. She didn't even speak; she went straight to the closet and began removing the items from the bags. While doing so, she heard the TV cut off and knew an unwanted conversation was about to take place. Tired of arguing, she sighed and prepared herself for the confrontation.

"I love you, Layla," Darren expressed with sincerity.

Her body relaxed and she felt a surge deep in her belly. Layla walked out of the closet and acknowledged her husband.

"I love you, too, Darren."

Darren rose up from his comfortable position and responded, "So, if you love me, why are you fighting me on what I want to know?"

"Because I keep telling you it's nothing," Layla replied, releasing frustration.

"Look, I thought about it, and I feel like I was wrong to involve a lawyer. So, I apologize."

His words soothed her soul as she sat down on her side of the bed to finish the conversation.

"Apology accepted," Layla said, then leaned in to kiss him.

Their lips locked and turned from a light kiss to a slight tongue-wrestling match. After the brief interlocking of tongues, Darren switched the subject.

"So what were the bags for?"

"Oh, you know it's that time of the month when me and my friends have ladies' night."

"Well, what if I said I made plans for me and you to be together?"

In an attempt to stop herself from getting frustrated, Layla sighed.

"Darren, you know me and my friends only go out once a month. So why are you tripping?"

Not liking her response, he gave her a blank stare. Layla read his facial expression and knew what was coming next.

"So you're going to choose your friends over me?"

Layla exhaled. "No, but don't do this right now. We just apologized to each other, and I don't want to start another argument."

"Okay, we won't," Darren said and turned away from her like a little kid having a slight tantrum from not getting his way.

Layla shook her head at the sight of her husband acting like a seven-year-old. She quickly went into seductive mode.

"Darren, turn on your back," she whispered in his ear.

"Huh?"

"You heard me," Layla said as she began peeling off her clothes.

"What are you—"

Darren couldn't even finish his sentence; his lips were met with her finger.

"Shhh, don't speak right now. Just listen," Layla whispered seductively while removing his article of clothing from the waist down.

As he watched her take hold of his manhood, he became instantly aroused. From her actions, he knew he was in for a treat. Layla moved slowly, making sure to pay extra attention to each detail. Kisses rained down on him from head to pelvis as she moved her tongue in a seductive circular motion. Enjoying the encounter, Darren moaned deeply and returned the pleasure as he gently caressed her silhouette while playing in her wet-box.

Now fully into the mood, they kissed each other passionately. They both could feel the love as they shared each other's energy. Slow and steady, they made love like they didn't want it to end.

After consuming each other's bodies, Darren fell asleep, while Layla jumped up to go into the bathroom to freshen up. She stopped to admire her thickness in front of the mirror and went into deep thought, weighing her options.

Either I go out, have fun, and suffer the consequences later with Darren, or deprive myself and let him control me. I already got my outfit, so why waste it?

Layla made her mind up as she turned on the shower and got ready for divas' night out.

*****

Eric and Deseree were at the law firm working on a high-profile case, which involved a well-known, respected businessman who had ties with some unsavory types. He decided money laundering wasn't enough. He had to get involved in drugs, extortion, and murder. Deseree hated dealing with clients like him, but she had to do what she had to do to make her paper.

Eric walked in looking tired and beat down from the all-nighter he had trying to find out what kind of dirt Chance had on him. He walked over to his desk and picked up the phone to check his voicemail. Eric's face displayed a look of boredom as he quietly listened to the automated voice on the other end of the phone. As he yawned and continued to listen, he went into his desk drawer and pulled out a photo of Trevor that made him smile. He thought to himself, *Damn, I miss you.*

Then, he looked over at the photo of him and Dereseé sitting on his desk and shook his head in shame. Eric truly loved his wife, but it was something about his jump off that had him sprung. He sighed and returned back to his work.

A few minutes later, he overheard Dereseé talking. Judging from the sound of her voice, Dereseé felt uneasy.

Michelle strolled into Dereseé's office and greeted her with a huge smile.

"Hey, girl! I just came by to check up on you. How are you doing?" Michelle asked.

Dereseé's voice trembled as she tried to mask her true feelings.

"I'm doing about as well as can be expected. I went to see Chance to find out what dirt he had on Eric. Girl, you won't believe what he told me."

Michelle's heart raced. She had left Chance unconscious and didn't know how he managed after she stole his file and left him for dead. She also feared he had told Dereseé about their encounter.

Michelle felt a huge lump in her throat and got a strange vibe as Dereseé began talking. For the first time, she felt guilty about what she had done and what she planned to do. She ruined her friend's life.

I can't do this, she thought to herself. *I have to tell her.*

"Dessie," Michelle interrupted, "I've got to tell you something."

Before Michelle could finish her confession, they were startled by the sound of footsteps coming down the hall toward them. Eric appeared in the doorway of Deseree's office and leaned on the doorframe.

"Oh, what's going on, Michelle? I didn't know that was you," Eric said.

"Eric," Michelle replied, greeting him.

The tension was so thick it couldn't be cut with a chainsaw. There was a period of awkward silence.

The look of guilt on Michelle's face was replaced by anger as she remembered why she came to the office in the first place. They quickly changed the subject to keep Eric from picking up on their conversation about him and Trevor.

"Well, I gotta go, girl. I'll see you later on tonight. Cocktales, right?" Michelle said enthusiastically.

Deseree tried to return the enthusiasm. "You know it. I'll be ready. Can't wait."

The two friends hugged, and Michelle watched Deseree brush past Eric and disappear deep into the office. Eric and Michelle stood in a brief faceoff. Anger brewed in the pit of her stomach. Without a word, Eric turned away, walked back to his office, and closed the door.

Michelle rummaged through her purse and pulled out an envelope. She looked around to make certain no one was watching. As Michelle made her exit, she stopped in front of Eric's mailbox and dropped the envelope in.

"It's on, bitch," she mumbled while walking out the door.

After several hours of reviewing depositions and making phone calls, Dereeé walked into Eric's office and told him, "I'm leaving. Don't forget I'm meeting the girls tonight for cocktails, so I'll be home late."

Eric looked up from his computer and noticed the worried look on Dereeé's face. With concern, he asked, "You alright, babe? You don't look so good. You sure you want to still try to go out tonight? How about I pick up some of your favorite takeout and we chill at home?"

"I'm fine," she replied. "Just worried about this case, that's all. I'm actually looking forward to tonight. I need something to take my mind off work."

Eric wasn't convinced, but he didn't continue to push.

"Okay. I'll see you later then."

"Yeah," Dereeé replied.

Eric rose from his chair and began approaching Dereeé. She quickly exited the office before he could get close enough to touch her. He put his hand on his head in frustration. He heard Dereeé moving around as she gathered her things. The sound of her footsteps echoed like the beat of a drum as she hurried for the front door.

Eric walked out to the lobby of the office to make sure everything was locked down before returning to his office to continue working. That's when he noticed an envelope hanging out of his office mailbox. He took it out and opened it. In an instant, his mood softened as he read.

Heeey, Daddy! Meet me at our favorite spot tonight. I have a special guest I know you'll like. Trust me, it will be well worth it. Don't keep me

128

waiting, and don't forget to stop and get my Café Breva before you come. You know I like it hot and steamy. Love you, Daddy…Trevor… XOXO

Eric quickly forgot about work, Deseré, and the information Chance held over him. His manhood began to stiffen at the thought of the surprise Trevor had for him. Eric went back to his office to freshen up in the washroom adjacent to his desk. Then he packed up his things and left to rendezvous with Trevor.

The day for ladies' night out finally arrived. Sanai went into her closest and pulled out three outfits she would choose from to wear that night. She wanted the outfit to complement to the red-bottom shoes she had borrowed from Layla. When she looked inside the box to admire them, she stumbled upon a pretty decorated book. She examined the book cover that had hearts and smiley faces drawn on it. Sanai chuckled out loud at the childish drawings.

Squinting her eyes, she turned it over to the back cover. Sanai smiled when she realized that she held the book she had been waiting to read ever since she first saw Layla writing inside it in her office. Her eyes lit up like a kid in a candy store. She cracked open the diary, and to her surprise, a picture of her and Layla fell out. She briefly looked down to the floor at the picture and then at the book.

Sanai began skimming through the beginning of *B.F.F.* A smile formed on her face once she read the dedication to her and King on the first page. She thought the perfect time to read the book was while she was taking a bath. Just as she was about to walk into the bathroom to run her water, her phone ringing interrupted her.

"Hey, Layla."

"Hey," Layla replied softly.

"Girl, why are you whispering?" Sanai asked, while walking to the bathroom and turning on the water.

Peeping out of her bathroom, Layla answered, "Darren wants me to stay home, but I done fucked him senseless. So, he's asleep. That means I'm stepping out."

Sanai laughed at her best friend sounding like her. "Girl, you're crazy. Why doesn't he want you to come, though?"

"Oh, I didn't tell you? He read some of my diary and took it the wrong way."

Sanai glanced over at the book that was sitting on her bed.

"Look, Lay, I'm 'bout to get in the bath and get ready for tonight. I'm sure you'll tell me all about everything tonight."

"I sure will. See you soon," Layla said before hanging up.

Suddenly, Sanai was interested in the diary more than before. Anxious to read what caused Darren to get mad, she took the diary in the bathroom to read during her bath before she got dressed to enjoy ladies' night out.

Cocktales

Let the Stories Begin

Sanai weaved through traffic like a racecar driver. After cursing like a sailor at all the cab drivers that held her up, she finally made a left into the parking lot at 3rd and Market. Her destination was Positano Coast Lounge where she knew her best friends were waiting on her. And knowing them like the back of her hand, she was the topic of discussion due to her being fashionably late. The contents of Layla's diary had her tripping, and she was not ready to deal with her.

She hopped out her maroon X6 and cat walked over to the entrance. Sanai had an ass that could stop traffic.

Over top of all the horns beeping and clicking of Gucci heels, she heard someone yell out, "Chocolate!"

The light turned red, causing her to pause at the corner and turn around to see who was trying to get her attention. Through her Gucci lenses, she spotted the heckler jogging up to her. She sighed while waiting for whatever was about to transpire. By the way he was dressed, she could already tell he was definitely not her type.

"Miss, you dropped your keys," the man said.

"Thank you," Sanai replied nonchalantly while reaching out to take them from his hand.

She thought he was trying to holla at her, but she was wrong.

Before walking away, though, the man told her, "Let me not hold you up so ya man won't be waiting any longer."

Sanai chuckled and then responded, "I don't have one of those and for your information, I'm here to meet up with my girlfriends. But, thanks again."

"Oh, you're welcome, sexy."

Not wanting to lead the man on, she continued walking. She was far from lacking self-confidence and could even be a little conceited at times, so his remark about her being sexy definitely wasn't needed.

After entering The Positano Coast Restaurant, Sanai turned left and proceeded to where her girlfriends Desereé, Layla, and Michelle were waiting at a reserved table on the deck. She smiled while thinking back on how fate had brought them all together. These self-made divas had met at a women's convention. Best friends Sanai and Layla were in attendance, and the same went for Deseree and Michelle. They were assigned to the same table, clicked immediately, and had been friends ever since. At that particular event, they made a vow to always have divas' night out one Friday out of each month. Three years later, they continued the tradition despite Dereseé and Layla having significant others. Sanai and Michelle were the single ones between the four of them.

Since the girls wanted to switch it up, they chose the new Positano Coast Restaurant in Old City Philly as their spot. It was known for their lavish surroundings, sexy seafood dishes, and exotic cocktails. Their alcohol consumption helped the conversation turn from casual to x-rated. Everything from oral sex to threesomes was discussed as they danced and shot the breeze over cocktails.

Sanai was pleasantly surprised. The pictures on the Internet did not capture the real beauty of the establishment. As she walked across the beautiful deck, she could see Dereseé and Layla waving from a gorgeous white cabana positioned adjacent to the restaurant's oversized window. The white sheer curtains surrounding the cabana blew gently from the evening breeze.

Like always, Layla was the first to greet her.

"There's my favorite diva. 'Bout time you got here."

Trying not to seem like she knew Layla's most inner thoughts, Sanai played along. "Well, you know me… I always got to be fashionably late," Sanai said, while showing off her Gucci footwear.

"Oh, where did you get them from?" Not giving Sanai a chance to respond, Layla added, "I guess my red bottoms weren't good enough, huh?"

Sanai flashed Layla a half grin without answering.

After all the ooh's, aww's, and admiration of the fly shoes, Dereseé asked the question everyone wanted to know.

"Where did you get them? They look just like the ones I showed Eric that I wanted for my birthday." Dereseé smiled and then held up her half-finished cocktail. "Great divas think alike!"

Taken off guard by her comment, Sanai recovered quickly with a spin.

"I don't know, 'cause I didn't buy them. I owe these to what's between my thick thighs."

"I heard that," Dereseé said, giving her a high-five twice.

"So what ya'll drinking?" Sanai asked, while surveying the table in search of hers.

"Rum Runners, and calm down. Yours is on the way. We were trying to wait for you and Michelle," Layla said, getting the attention of the waitress.

"Cool. Are we doing the usual where everybody buys a round?" Sanai inquired.

Everybody agreed. Just then, her drink arrived and she proceeded to take a sip.

"Well, I hope Michelle hurries up," Sanai said, while holding her glass up to imitate toasting.

Sanai did what she had done since the day her life changed—live in the moment and act as if things did not bother her. The more uncomfortable or in pain she was, the more she turned the fun dial up. She tried to shake off what she had discovered in Layla's diary as she went into full acting mode.

"Mmm, this is good. I'm gonna need a lot of these tonight. I see we're gonna have a good time," Sanai said, while waving her right arm in the air.

Beyoncé's "Who Run The World" blared through the speakers, causing everyone at the table to wave their arms in the air, as well.

"The DJ must have known I stepped in the building," Sanai said as she got up holding her drink and proceeded to the small dance area by the DJ booth.

The rest of the clan followed her so they could dance to the ladies anthem. Once they finished, they returned to the table. That's when Sanai asked the very question that was asked every time they met up for divas' night out.

"So who wants to tell the first story?"

Everybody was quiet.

"Don't play shy now, bitches. Okay, I guess I will start it off then," Sanai said, then took another sip of her drink. "Before I start, let me ask y'all, what was your experience like the first time you had phone sex?"

Not one to discuss her sexual romps freely, Layla surprised everyone by answering first.

"Okay, bear with me y'all. It was my senior year in college, and I was dating this guy named Jeff...and let me add the sex was the shit." Layla giggled before continuing. "We went on break for the winter. I was horny as hell, and he had called me one late night talking 'bout how hard he was. He was talking so dirty he had my walls feeling like the Atlantic Ocean. He expressed how he wanted me to sit on his face and how bad he wanted to taste me. Well, while he was telling me all that, I started rubbing myself and moaning. At first, I was embarrassed, but he encouraged the session and started to please himself, too.

We even exploded at the same time. It was the best phone sex I ever had."

"Wow, I need to go to the ladies' room and wipe myself," Sanai said jokingly.

The ladies broke out into laughter.

"Okay, who's next?" Sanai asked while looking at Desereé.

"My first time was so wack that it ain't even worth speaking about. The dude definitely wasn't like Jeff," Desereé said, trying to stay upbeat but thinking about how shitty her life was.

*****

After sitting in traffic for almost an hour and waiting in line for coffee for twenty minutes, Eric was finally on his way to spend the night with someone who knew exactly what he wanted and how he wanted it. He drove down Route 38 in New Jersey. The setting sun gave the sky a beautiful amber hue. He took a deep breath as he turned into the parking lot. Excitement took over his entire body in anticipation of what lay ahead.

He walked to the door, turned the knob, and walked inside. The room was dimly lit with soft music playing in the background. Eric grew even more excited. He put down his keys and the coffee on the table as he continued to scan the room. Eric called out for Trevor.

"Babe! Babe! Where are you? I got your Café Breva."

There was no answer.

"C'mon out and let Daddy see your sexy ass. I've been waiting for this."

Suddenly, Eric felt a sharp pinch in the side of his neck that came from behind.

"What the hell?"

After about five seconds, Eric started to feel lightheaded. His legs felt like rubber, and the room began spinning as he slumped to the floor.

An hour passed and Eric began to stir. He woke up to find himself naked and handcuffed to a chair. Looking at him was a woman dressed in a leather mask, leather and barbed wire bra and panties, and stilettos that made her look like a giant.

In a deep voice, she said, "Like my surprise?"

"What the fuck is going on? Where's Trevor?" Eric replied in a soft, groggy voice.

"Oh, you didn't hear? Trevor is in the hospital being treated for trying to kill himself because of a slimy motherfucker like you!"

"What the fuck are you talking about? Trevor left a letter in my office that said he was meeting me here."

Just then, an iced-out whip cracked across his back.

"Did I give you permission to speak?"

"Bitch, I don't know what you're up to, but if you don't get these handcuffs off me…"

Just then, the woman put her boot in Eric's crotch. Her spiked heel pressed firmly against his scrotum. Eric let out a manly groan as the pain radiated all over his body.

"You know, there are two things I can't stand. The first is you. The second is being threatened. I don't respond well to threats!"

The woman pressed her heel into his sack even harder. Then, she took a scarf and tied it across his mouth.

"All you down low brothers think you can walk around having your cake and eating it, too. You don't give a shit about the people you hurt. All you care about is yourself. Well, guess what? That's going to end today. Because of your nasty ass, you've hurt two people who will have to endure a lifetime of pain because you couldn't keep your dick in your pants!"

Eric's eyes grew wide.

"Yeah, playa, you know what I'm talking about. I would tell you to go get tested for HIV, but that won't be necessary," the woman said with a chuckle.

She reached for the files, which contained all the evidence of his infidelity, including Trevor's test results she took from the hospital. She turned toward him, threw it at him, and then spat in his face.

Hoping to find a way to break free from this bondage, Eric moved frantically in the chair. The woman took the butt of the whip and struck him across his face, dazing him. Then, she grabbed another scarf and wrapped it around his neck, causing him to gasp for air. After his breathing became labored due to his short air supply, the woman let go and slowly walked around Eric like a mighty warrior. Leaning down in front of him, she removed her mask as she grabbed a handful of the bulge between his legs. The look of surprise and horror on Eric's face made her wet with satisfaction.

She smiled and said, "I'm sorry, but your appointment to get your tired, little dick sucked by your man-whore has been cancelled."

She walked behind him again, reached into her medicine bag, and pulled out another syringe that contained a hefty dose of an anesthetic only used in the hospital under the watchful eye of an anesthesiologist. Tears streamed down his face as Eric tried to plead for mercy through his bondage. His words were muffled. All that could be heard clearly was, "Michelle, please don't do this..."

Eric attempted to make a final plea for his life. Then, he felt another sharp pain in his neck, and his head slowly began to drop. She walked back around to look him in the eyes as life slowly left his body.

Without an ounce of remorse, Michelle said, "You fucked with my friend. Now, I'm fucking with you. Rest in hell, bitch."

Michelle watched until Eric took one last deep breath. Then, she untied him, and with all the strength she had, she dragged his limp, naked body to the bed. She put on her gloves and began to clean up any traces of her ever being there. She changed into her brand-new party dress and pumps, picked up her belongings, and headed for the door. She turned around and scanned the room, making sure she didn't leave anything behind. She forgot one last thing. After walking to the bed where Eric's body lay, she dropped an open bottle of pills on the bed so they could scatter around him. She then left a note next to the pillow that read:

My life was just a big lie. I couldn't bear living and looking at the people I love knowing I've caused them so much pain. So, I did them all a favor and sacrificed myself with the hope of ending their misery. I pray in time they will find it in their hearts to forgive me. —Eric

Michelle was always good at forging people's signatures. After studying Eric's handwriting over the years, she had it down to a science.

She walked to the door and closed it behind her. She walked next door to another parking lot where her car was parked, got in, and looked at her watch.

"Shit! I'm late."

She started the car to head back to Philly where she would join her girls for cocktails.

Before pulling off, she sent Desereé a text. *I'm running late, Diva. Will be there soon. Love you.*

Michelle put on her Prada shades and threw her whip in gear. She pulled out of the parking lot as if nothing happened. Her only agitation was running late for her evening out with the girls. She pondered how she would break the news to Desereé about needing to be tested for HIV because of her husband's double dipping on the down low. She was still curious as to who the unidentified woman was in the pictures from the file she stole from Chance. Nevertheless, feelings of vindication filled her heart as she headed to meet her girls for food, fun, and fantasy.

*****

Back at Positano Coast, Layla took another sip of her drink and said, "We need to wait for Michelle anyway, especially for our big stories."

Sanai stood to her feet and twirled around. "Awww, y'all are wack," she said, while flagging the both of them. She then took another sip of her Rum Runner and continued on.

Feeling the effects of her three drinks, Layla leaned in close to Sanai, who gave her a strange look and urged the ladies to order another drink on her as she excused herself from the table.

"Ladies, I'll be right back. I hope Michelle magically appears so we can keep it flowing."

As Sanai walked away, the two ladies summoned the waitress. The waitress acknowledged them with a head nod while taking care of another table.

Desereé retrieved her cell phone from her purse and tapped the screen to call Michelle. When the screen illuminated, the message alert symbol was in the center of her phone. Desereé opened up the text message that was from Michelle explaining she was running late. After placing her phone back in her purse, she proceeded to enjoy her girls that were present.

Sanai returned from the back of the lounge still prancing and singing.

Desereé took the last sip of her drink, then looked up and told Sanai, "Oh, I got a message from Michelle. She's late, of course, but should be here soon. So, let's keep the fun rolling."

The waitress appeared at the cabana just as Sanai was about to go in on a story. "What else can I get you?" she asked in a polite voice.

Sanai held up her right index finger and crossed her legs as she began to speak. "We—"

Deseree cut her off in mid-sentence. "We would like to change our drink order. We would like three Positano Lemon Drops and two large orders of your Stuffed Peruvian Scallops."

Sitting back, Sanai responded, "Thanks for giving us some flavor. Now let me continue what I started before my brief tour."

She was eager to jump into her story.

"I asked y'all that question because it leads into my story of one of my coworker's first time."

"Cool. Let the story begin," Deseree chimed in, preparing her mind for the craziness she was sure Sanai was about to share.

Sanai took one more sip and then allowed the words to fall from her supple lips...

The 1st Timer

Alliesha Goodwin was overwhelmed with work, sighing as she steadily typed away. Being a receptionist in the Penn Health System, this was expected during her eight to five shift. With her face glued to the computer and her fingers going to work, she didn't notice she was putting on a free peek show for the male staff. Even some of the females were enjoying the sight. One after another, housekeepers and janitors on her floor walked past drooling at the sight of her nipples poking out of her shirt from the cold hospital air. One worker in particular, whom she didn't care for, was the first to speak about the nipple sighting.

"Hey, Alliesha. You must be happy to see me," Donyell, one of the housekeepers, said.

"Why would I be happy to see you? You know I don't like you," she replied, rolling her eyes in disgust.

"Or could it be that you were anticipating my arrival?" Donyell continued, leaning in to get a closer view.

Donyell leaning in was a dead giveaway, and looking down, Alliesha saw what everybody else was staring at. She quickly threw on her sweater, raining on everybody's parade.

"It's too late for that. I already got my peek on."

"Shut up, Donyell, and get your dirty ass away from my desk. Go mop a bathroom or something."

"You're a hater"

"Whatever," Alliesha said, while waving him away at the same time.

Five minutes later, the sound of a linen cart could be heard coming down the hall. This could only mean one thing to Alliesha; her crush, Mikell Graves, was on his way. Every time she heard the cart, she imagined him pushing the cart around the corner and appearing naked. Then picking her up, taking her into the patient bathroom, and bending her over in the bathroom stall.

She finally snapped out of her fantasy world and quickly took off the sweater, feeling that Mikell was the only one worthy enough to get a peek at her nipples. The cart sounds stopped, giving her time to harden them by rubbing her fingertips on them. While she perked them up, the cart sounds got closer and then a slim, handsome, brown-skinned man appeared.

"Hey, Mikell," she said in a sweet, seductive way.

"What's up, Alliesha?"

"You know, you're in my presence."

Mikell laughed at her remark and then replied, "Speaking of which, I see I'm not the only one that's up."

"What do you mean?" Alliesha asked, letting his reply go over her head.

Mikell didn't answer. Instead, he let his eyes do all the talking. Alliesha followed them and then let out a chuckle. Her plan to get his full attention finally worked. Now all she had to do was keep it that way. Every day she always had a trick up her sleeve, whether it was bending over while he passed or something as small as sticking a pen in her mouth while they had short conversation. When it came down to it, the nipple trick was the icebreaker.

"You always putting on a peep show for me," Mikell said.

"Don't act like you don't like it," Alliesha shot back.

"Oh, I see you got to peep those missiles, too, Mikell," Donyell said, almost killing the spark between them.

"Donyell, take your nosy ass someplace. Matter of fact, empty my trash while us grown folks converse," Alliesha told him.

"It's cool. We got work to do," Mikell interrupted before a verbal confrontation could start. He then leaned in and told her, "We'll finish this conversation later. I promise."

Mikell's words brought heat back into the atmosphere and even between her thighs from the way he whispered the words. Alliesha smiled, showing off her pearly whites and signaling that Mikell scored a touchdown. Mikell knew she was wide open, so he decided to score some extra points.

"Look, why don't we stop playing games with each other? I know I like you and vice versa, so what's up with you giving me the number?"

Finally, Alliesha thought to herself as she tore a piece a paper off her sticky pad and wrote down her number. She didn't want to say it out loud because Donyell looked like he had his antennas up high. As she passed her number to Mikell, she still had the Kool-aid smile she bore from earlier when he whispered to her.

"And don't hesitate to call me either," Alliesha said while he stored her number in his phone.

"Trust me, I won't," Mikell responded as he rolled the cart away to continue working.

Due to both of them being engulfed with work, they weren't able to speak to each other again during the rest of the workday. At 4:50 p.m., Alliesha prepared to leave, collecting all of her possessions. Her phone vibrated as a text came through. As she began reading it, she started to grin from ear to ear. It was from Mikell; he stated he would contact her later on in the day.

Alliesha was anxious while awaiting Mikell's phone call. When she arrived home, she checked her phone after she cooked, while she ate, and even after getting out the shower. Since she kept her phone on vibrate, she always checked to see if anybody contacted her, but this time, she was waiting on one in particular. But, after the shower, she kind of gave up on receiving a call from Mikell. She just lay back wrapped in a towel and decided to take her mind off of him.

While watching her favorite TV show Law & Order, her phone began to vibrate. It was Mikell texting her to see what she was doing. Alliesha quickly responded by texting back: Nothing, just watching my favorite TV show. *He texted her back:* I apologize for taking so long. *Alliesha texted back:* You don't have to apologize.

Being a freak, without hesitation, Mikell decided to get straight to the point and asked her what she was wearing at the time. Alliesha grinned at the text before quickly typing that she only had on a towel. But, then, she went into detail about how her nipples were hard and being somewhat horny.

Mikell's eyes lit up when that text came across his phone. His penis began to rise, as well. His plan worked like a charm…and fast, too. After what she sent via text, he decided to call her. When Alliesha received the call, she decided to play with his mind. So, she sent him straight to voicemail. He called right back only to get the same result. She chuckled at the fact he didn't know what was going on, but on the third call, she answered.

"I guess calling three times is a charm," Mikell said after she picked up.

"I guess so. I see I got your attention."

"Yes, you do, and do you want to know what else you have standing at attention?"

Alliesha moaned at the thought of knowing how hard his dick was.

"Sounds nice, Mikell," she responded.

"Alliesha, let me ask you a question."

"You can ask me anything you want, baby," she replied seductively.

"Did you ever have phone sex before?"

"No."

"Well, would you like for me to be your first?"

She hesitated at first and then answered, "Umm, okay."

"Cool. Well, let's get started," Mikell said.

He was already naked and rubbing his erection. He told her to take off the towel so she could be naked, too. After removing the towel from her body, she put her phone on speaker and started to rub on her nipples. She became aroused as she began to moan...

Layla stopped her in the middle of the story.

"Wow! She told you all that?" Layla asked, looking confused.

Sanai could detect Layla's doubt about the story and cleared her throat.

"Yeah, girl. I was surprised with all the details, too, and while she was sharing it with me, I kept saying, 'T.M.I., girl. T.M.I.'."

Layla knew the story was about Sanai, but who was the dude and why lie? She wasn't hesitant to put her on blast.

"Bitch, you know that story was all you," Layla spat. "I don't know why you fronting."

If it weren't for Sanai being dark skin, everybody would have seen her turn beet red from being embarrassed by Layla putting her on the spot. She didn't fold under the pressure, though. She just shot Layla an evil glare and then acted like nothing was ever said about her story.

Not knowing why the two were disagreeing, Desereé excused herself and walked to the ladies' room. After entering the restroom, Desereé went straight for the sink. She leaned in and took a gander at her reflection in the mirror. She had her own secrets and wanted so badly to be rid of them.

*****

Back at the table, Sanai decided to find out what was on Layla's mind. She wanted to know why she put her on the spot the way she did.

"Look, Layla, if you got something to get off ya chest, now's the time."

Layla stared at her best friend with a blank look, but didn't answer. Sanai sighed before speaking again.

"I know you ain't still trippin' about what took place between me, you, and your husband. I told you that I only did it to fulfill my sexual desire and save your marriage. It was only pure entertainment, nothing more. I still look at you as my best friend, and I hope you still look at me the same."

Layla's heart skipped a beat when Sanai mentioned their encounter. She was embarrassed that Sanai would even speak of it in this manner. Layla cleared her throat trying to recover from the hard blow.

"No, I'm not tripping. I'm sorry if you felt like I put you on the spot, but I knew you were talking about yourself in that story, that's all. Why lie about the story being someone else?"

A little jealous about the story, Layla sat there staring at her appetizer. Sanai just looked at her, not answering her question.

While on her way back to the table, Dereseé paid attention to what seemed to be Sanai and Layla indulging in a heated debate. Since she noticed, she spoke on it right when she sat down.

"Hey, is everything good over here?"

Sanai smiled and spoke first, trying to change the subject.

"Yeah, girl, everything is good. Just had to clear the air with Layla, that's all."

"Okay. Layla, what about you? Is everything good?" Dereseé asked, playing detective.

Layla sat back, folded her arms, and crossed her right leg over her left. "Yeah, everything is good," Layla replied, even though her body language said otherwise.

"Girl, unfold them arms and get rid of that attitude. Don't be a party pooper," Sanai said with a fake smile.

"I know, right? Plus, I see our drinks are on the way over here," Dereseé said, changing the mood.

When the cocktail waitress came with their next round, she had her eyes square on Sanai's shoes and then her face.

"Excuse me for staring so hard, but you look very familiar. I know you from somewhere."

"You must have me mistaken with someone else, because this is my first time here."

The waitress took a closer look and then it dawned on her where she had seen Sanai.

"Yeah, it's you. You were with that handsome man who gave me that hefty tip over at Cuba Libre."

The waitress's comment made everybody's antennas go up. Layla was the first to comment.

"Ooh, girl, spill the beans. What, you had a hot date over at Cuba Libre?"

Sanai shot Layla another nasty look before saying, "Look, could you please let it go, Miss. It sounds like you're trying to hit on me. I know I'm sexy and all, but I'm strictly dickly."

The waitress kindly turned around and walked away, taking the insult on the chin so she wouldn't put her job in jeopardy.

"I see you got a lot of fans," Dereseé commented after the waitress left.

"Yeah, well that's what you get when you're as sexy as me," Sanai said with cockiness.

Layla was convinced Sanai had plenty to hide and did not like the shade she was throwing her way. She was sick of it and knew just how to address it. She was not used to the new secretive Sanai. Layla sat back in her seat and drank her cocktail straight down.

"Damn, girl, you're not playing," Dereseé said, her eyes widening.

Sanai and Dereseé raised their glasses as Sanai yelled, "Bottoms up!"

Layla smiled and went in for the kill. "Well, my story for the night is anything but ordinary. So, y'all might want to order another cocktail."

Sanai didn't know what Layla was up to and was concerned about her behavior. Layla order a round of Patrón shots and they arrived a short while later. The ladies retrieved the tall shot glasses from the mirrored tray. They all laughed as Layla held the glass up and shouted, "Salute!" Then they threw their heads back and swallowed.

Leaning in, Layla planted a kiss on Sanai's lips. "Now here we go."

Everyone except Sanai leaned in listening intently as Layla's story began.

"It was a few months ago…"

Happy Anniversary

Darren walked into his house after a hard day at work. Once inside, he noticed candles and rose petals leading to the dining room, setting the mood. His wife, Layla, forewarned him that he was in for a surprise, but he didn't know what was in store when he walked in.

He took off his suit jacket, loosened his tie, and walked over to the closet to put his briefcase inside. As he opened the door, a piece of paper fell, catching him off guard. He put his briefcase inside, closed the closet, and then picked the paper up. Once he began reading, a huge grin formed on his face. It was instructions on what to do once he arrived.

Darren followed the first step, which instructed him to go to the dining room and sit down. He noticed a big bottle of Rosé on ice inside a bucket. A champagne glass was to the side of it, along with every utensil set, just like in a restaurant. He then glanced over the paper again and followed the next instruction.

"Waitress, I'm ready to be served," Darren yelled out.

Layla appeared dressed in a sexy maid outfit and stilettos, carrying a plate of steak, broccoli, and potatoes.

"Here's ya food, sir. Your wife will be down shortly," Layla said, role-playing.

Darren smiled. "Oh, okay. We're role-playing."

Layla held in her laughter and spoke again as his servant. "Anything else you need before I go?"

"Yes. Could you pour me a glass of champagne?" Darren answered.

Layla followed his orders and poured him a glass.

"Thank you, miss. Now can you tell my wife I'm waiting for her," Darren said as he opened up his napkin containing the eating utensils.

"I will gladly go get her while you enjoy your dinner," Layla replied, then went upstairs.

Darren cut into his juicy steak that was smothered in A-1 Sauce just like he liked it. After eating a piece, he ate some of his potatoes and broccoli. Then he washed it down with a sip of Rosé.

"Now this is good," he said to himself as he continued digging into his meal.

Five minutes later, he heard footsteps coming from the staircase. He turned around as the footsteps turned into heel clicks. His eyes grew wide at the sight of his wife stepping in with a red laced bra and panty set from Fredrick's Of Hollywood and wearing the same stilettos she had on with the maid outfit. Her voluptuous curves excited Darren. Sporting her size thirteen in all the right places, Layla could have been a plus-size model.

She walked over to him and planted a juicy kiss on his lips, then hugged him tightly.

"Happy anniversary," Layla said in a sexy drawl.

Darren picked her up and placed her in his lap.

"Happy anniversary, babe," Darren replied while caressing her thighs like he loved to do whenever she straddled him.

"Are you enjoying your food?"

"Yes, I am. Are you going to eat with me?"

"No, baby. I already ate. I'm waiting on dessert," Layla said as she got up and poured herself a glass of champagne.

With his wife looking so sexy, Darren couldn't keep his eyes off her. Layla caught him staring and blushed.

"Eat ya food before it gets cold," Layla told him, then took a sip of champagne.

She sat next to him while he ate and began massaging his right leg leading up to his manhood. Instantly, he started to become stiff inside his pants.

"You're going to enjoy yourself tonight, baby," Layla whispered in his ear as she unzipped his pants.

Steaming with desire, she massaged his erection. Darren found it hard to eat and receive sexual caresses from Layla. So, he put his fork down and took a sip of his champagne. After he sat his glass down, Layla went under the table and began going to work orally. Darren lifted the tablecloth so he, too, could enjoy the show his wife was putting on. He watched as she took in his whole manhood without choking.

Two minutes later, she rose and whispered in his ear, "You ready to go upstairs for the real show?"

"Oh yeah, let's go," Darren said as he got up and started unbuttoning his shirt.

Layla grabbed his hand and guided him upstairs to their bedroom. As they entered the red-lighted room, Darren spotted another woman lying in their bed with the same outfit, but wearing a masquerade mask.

"What..."

Before he could finish, Layla shushed him and pulled him to the edge of their king-sized bed while the mystery woman got on all fours. Layla started removing his shirt while the mystery woman assisted with his pants. In no time, they had Darren standing in his birthday suit. Layla kissed on his chest while the other woman licked and sucked his member softly. She was just as good as Layla, if not better, making him grab her hair and guide her motions. Layla then slid down his chest and joined in while the woman assisted her by slipping his penis into her mouth. Darren exhaled as Layla began where she left off at the dinner table.

A minute later, Darren pulled out of her mouth fully erect and ready to penetrate his wife. He placed her on her back, inserted himself, and put her legs on his shoulders. The other woman joined in by sucking Layla's nipples while Darren penetrated her. Layla was startled at first because the plan was to please Darren only. She had never been with a woman and hadn't planned on it. The more the woman tended to her, the more she began to enjoy every second. Her moans grew louder and louder. With the woman sucking her nipples and Darren hitting her G-spot with every stroke, she was unable to take it anymore and exploded.

After Layla's first eruption, they switched positions, with Darren lying on his back and Layla straddling him in a reverse cowgirl position. She bounced on him while his hands grasped her ass cheeks. The other woman sat and watched for a while, pleasuring herself before once again zeroing in on Layla's breasts. She sucked them as Layla displayed her rodeo skills. While being penetrated, kissed, and sucked all over, Layla felt another eruption coming. This time, she climaxed with a warning.

"Ooh, Sanai, keep sucking my nipples! I'm about to cum!"

Sanai followed her orders by taking one nipple into her mouth and playing with the other. Layla moved her hips, grinding deep until she felt Darren all the way inside her. Then she began shaking all over and letting out loud moans. The second one could have registered as a 3.5 on the Richter scale the way they had the bed shaking.

Once again, they switched positions. This time, Layla was bent over and Sanai lay on her back in front of Layla. Darren pushed the back of Layla's head until her face was in between Sanai's thighs. Not the one to ever be a carpet muncher, Layla was stuck, but soon, she found herself turned on by the way her best friend tasted. So, she took both hands, opened Sanai up, and began licking every inch, finding her way to the clitoris. Turned on by the sight, Darren increased the speed up his strokes while smacking Layla on her ass. Sanai moaned out and told her how well she was performing.

"Ooh yeah, girl, keep that tongue right there."

Layla felt Darren growing larger and harder inside her, and she knew he was on the verge of his first ejaculation. By the time he announced that he was cumming, Layla had Sanai moaning and shaking from her licking. Sweat covered everyone as they found a spot individually on the bed to catch their breath. By this time, Sanai was no longer wearing her mask, and

Darren could finally identify the mystery woman. He didn't say a word about it. All he knew was his wife satisfied him just the way he wanted on their fifth anniversary.

Dereseé sat straight up as the last word escaped Layla's lips. She could tell Sanai was not happy with her sharing that story. Sanai yelled out in anger.

"You bitch! After all my years of friendship, and you do this shit to me? You fucking freak! By the way, I read your little diary…and you're in love with me how? What the hell are you thinking? I like men. I only did that with you to spice shit up for you and your dry-ass husband. Get over it!"

Dereseé attempted to calm the pair down and remind them that they were in a public place. "Divas, please calm down. Y'all both are drunk, that's all. Talk about this shit later."

Sanai was not having it, though. She was out for blood. She couldn't believe Layla would betray her like that. As she stood to her feet, she stared down at Layla.

*****

Michelle gave new meaning to the word speeding as she tore across the Ben Franklin Bridge like Danica Patrick in Jay-Z's *Show Me What You Got* video. Surprisingly, all was quiet on the road, and she made it to Old City in record time without getting a ticket.

She parked her car, removed her sunglasses, and searched her purse for her makeup kit. Then she pulled down the sun visor and looked in the mirror to retouch her makeup. When she confirmed her makeup was flawless, she got out of the car and fixed her dress to make sure it fell just right over her sexy curves. She switched on her sexy diva walk and headed to the restaurant.

*****

Sanai went on and on until the waitress appeared with another round of shots.

"Hello, ladies. Is everything okay?" the waitress asked, while sitting the complimentary shots down.

Sanai went in again on the waitress. "Look, bitch, I told you that I don't like girls. We didn't order any more shots, so please stop reaching."

Sanai rolled her eyes at the waitress, and Layla sat back feeling like people could see her underwear. The waitress smiled at Dereseé before turning to face Sanai. Fed up with Sanai's smart remarks, she let her have it in a subtle way.

"Miss, I apologize if you think I'm bothering you, but that was not my intention. I'm just grateful for the fifty-dollar tip your man gave me before you two hurried to his truck. I will never forget the words he said to me about giving back because he was once a waiter."

The entire table looked at Sanai as the waitress walked away.

Suddenly, Dereseé jumped to her feet and yelled, "Bitch, how could you? You're a lowdown tramp!"

Now the one confused, Layla attempted to hold Dereseé back. Tears flowed down Dereseé's face as she put the puzzle together.

"I knew you had your skanky ways, but my fucking husband, Sanai? Are you that desperate that you would fuck your friend's husband?"

Usually loud and quick to speak, this time, Sanai said nothing. She just stared at Dereseé with cold eyes.

"What is she talking about, Sanai?" Layla asked. "Answer me!"

While staring at Layla, Dereseé yelled, "The man that the waitress just described is Eric. Ever since he made it, he's been leaving fifty-dollar tips and telling the server about how he, too, was a waiter once, so he always gives back. This bitch is cheating with my husband!"

Layla turned to face Sanai, who sat there still frozen. Just then, Dereseé lunged across the table and smacked Sanai so hard that she flipped out of her chair.

"You bitch!" Sanai shouted as she attempted to get up from the floor of the lounge.

The waitress and other staff rushed to assist the foursome. Still jumping and climbing over people, Dereseé continued.

"You bitter whore! Just because your man died years ago, it doesn't give you the right to have anybody's husband in sight. I'm gonna kill you!"

The words mixed with the mention of King's death ushered raging tears from the eyes of Sanai.

*****

As Michelle crossed the threshold, she began searching for her girls. Before she could ask anyone where they could be

157

found, Michelle heard elevated voices that sounded very much like Desereé and Layla.

"Damn, I must be missing a good story. Now, I gotta listen to their wisecracks about me being late first before getting a condensed version of the Cocktale that was being told."

Ready to make her grand entrance, Michelle turned the corner and raised her hands in the air as she bounced toward the table, but what she encountered was certainly less than pleasant.

"Heeey, Divas! Let's get the bottles poppin'! I finally…"

Michelle's grand entrance was sabotaged by yelling and death threats. She looked over and saw Desereé ready to lay hands on Sanai. Confused, Michelle rushed over to the table to find out what was going on. She stepped in front of Desereé as she prepared to go for a handful of Sanai's hair.

"Wait…wait…wait! Now just hold the hell on! Will somebody tell me what's going on here?"

Desereé's eyes were filled with rage and sadness as tears formed in her ducts.

"This bitch was fucking around with my husband! How could you betray me like that? I thought you were my girl! And you didn't just stop there. You had to go and turn out your best friend, too!"

Michelle's mouth gaped open in surprise. The missing piece of her puzzle had been found and put into place. The mystery woman in the pictures was Sanai. What she didn't know was Layla and Sanai were more than just best friends. It became clear to Michelle that Sanai was in the middle wherever there was drama.

"What the fuck? It was you? You were the bitch in the pictures!"

Michelle's words got the attention of all the ladies and a few other patrons who were trying to enjoy their evening. No sooner than those words left Michelle's lips, Desereé lunged forward, attempting to tear Sanai's head off. It took the efforts of Michelle and Layla to keep Desereé from succeeding in catching a case.

After the brief wrestling match at the table and threats of the police being called, Desereé said, "You know, I never understood why people always told me never allow your man around your friends. Now I know why. It's because of skanks like you!"

Then, she abruptly turned to Michelle with tear-filled eyes. Michelle's anger began to brew as her friend's life was broadcasted right in the middle of the restaurant. She didn't want to hurt Desereé, but due to the recent events, she had to find a way to tell her what she knew without telling her *how* she knew.

Michelle pulled Desereé aside to talk to her.

"Look, Dessie, I swear to you I knew nothing about Eric and Sanai. What I do know is that Eric was living foul. He was sneaking around with this young kid, Trevor. He came into the hospital with a gunshot wound to the face. I found out Trevor tried to commit suicide because he contracted HIV from his lover."

Michelle took a paper out of her bag that had the HIV results, handed it to Desereé, and then continued with her version of what happened.

159

"He kept talking about the time they spent together—business trips and kinky sexual encounters with him and other women. I found a picture of the three of them together outside of a hotel, but the image of the woman in the pictures was too blurry for me to make out who it was. It wasn't until I got here and heard all the drama that I realized the person in the pictures was Sanai. I would never do anything to hurt you. You should know that by now."

"Nooooo! Tell me it's not true, Micki!" Dereseé yelled out in agony, then collapsed into Michelle's arms and sobbed uncontrollably. "What am I going to do?"

For the first time, Michelle was vulnerable. She had no solution for the debacle that erupted during what was supposed to be a fun time with her girls. Michelle tried to hold back her tears and be strong for her friend. Knowing it was Sanai who Eric was sneaking around with made her skin turn red with anger, but what really made her sick to her stomach was knowing his sexual perversions put her friend in harm's way.

Suddenly, Dereseé pulled away from Michelle.

"I gotta get outta here! If I stay any longer, I'm going to kill that bitch. If she wants him that bad, she can have him. I have no more love for either of them. For all I care, they can both burn in hell!"

Dereseé and Michelle headed toward the door. Sanai and Layla were seated close by engaged in a heavy conversation. As they approached the pair, they could hear a non-apologetic Sanai gloating.

"She better had taken that bitch outta here or she would have had a big problem! It's not my fault her tight ass couldn't satisfy her man!"

Just then, Michelle's fist met Sanai's face with such force that it knocked her out of her chair. Gripping her by her clothes, she picked her up off the floor. A dazed Sanai slumped back down in the chair. She looked up at Michelle with a glazed look in her eyes. Layla was so stunned that she didn't know what to do.

Leaning into Sanai, Michelle said, "Now, it's my turn to tell my story…"

Michelle was at work one morning doing her rounds as usual, when she came across a young man lying in the bed with a hole the size of a quarter in his cheek. Being a compassionate doctor, she tended to her patient with care. When she reviewed the patient's file, it read that the cause for injury was an attempted suicide. After trying to offer her help, the little shit tried to reach up and choke her with her own stethoscope. To keep from fucking him up and losing her job, he was immediately sent to the psych floor for an evaluation.

Later, she went up to see the young man to get an update on his condition. When she walked into his room, he was heavily sedated and in restraints. When asked why he tried to take his own life, he told her it was because the man he loved was having his cake and eating it, too. He was married to a wonderful woman, but he was stepping out on her with him and some lowlife whore. Michelle watched the man try to bury his sorrows behind a blanket of tears, but there weren't enough tears in his body to soothe the sting he felt brought on by his reality. You see, the young man named Trevor entrusted his life to a man who left him with a package wrapped with a nice little bow. In it were three little letters…H I V! His lover's name was Eric, and the lowlife whore's name was Sanai.

Sanai and Layla looked at Michelle in horror.

Michelle grabbed Desereé's purse off the chair and started to walk away. Before she left, she turned around and said to them, "I bet your stories don't even come close to being as good as mine, bitches."

Desereé followed her friend's lead, but not before throwing the HIV results in Sanai's face. "I hope your romps with Eric were worth it, because the cocktails you'll be receiving will not be served at a bar. You perverted bitch, you just won HIV for a consolation prize."

Sanai bent down and picked up the paper that had Trevor and Eric's names along with the positive results.

"Oh my God! Nooooo!" Sanai screamed as she ran out of the lounge and headed to her car. Still dizzy from Michelle's handiwork, she fell and tripped the entire way.

Layla ran after her trying to console her, but she was too late. The only thing left behind was Sanai's shoe on the sidewalk as she pulled off at top speed. Layla ran in the street behind her and was almost hit by a car passing by.

Michelle assisted her friend in her pain. Desereé was in such a state of turmoil that she wasn't in any shape to drive. It was obvious this *Cocktales* night signified the end of an era for the four friends.

As they walked to her car, Michelle could hear the echo of sirens from Philadelphia's finest. She helped Desereé` inside. Desereé sat comatose in the front seat.

After getting in the car, Michelle looked at her friend and said, "Don't you worry about a thing. I'll take care of you. You're my girl. I always got your back no matter what."

Michelle then put the key in the ignition, shifted into drive, and drove off.

Chance of a Lifetime

Dereeé sat staring out of the window while tears continued to stream down her face. She could not believe her life had taken a turn for the worse. She had given Eric so much of her soul that she had nothing left to give. *Why* was the question that kept playing in her head. She was in such a daze that Dereeé didn't even realize how far Michelle had driven.

While driving, Michelle prepared herself to reveal the truth to her best friend.

Still staring out the window, Dereeé broke the silence. "Micki, I don't believe this. I should have listened. Damn, I should have listened."

Michelle leaned in and turned the stereo down. "Dessie, don't blame…"

She couldn't finish her sentence before Dereeé cut her off.

"No, Micki, don't do that. I have to own my shit. I know you mean well, but no, let me finish please," Dereeé yelled through sniffles.

Michelle followed her orders and continued to drive. She reached over and hit the windshield wiper button to clear the mist that had settled on the windows from the spring shower.

"Micki, I wasn't ready for what I was told, and I wrestled with it for the past two days. Why didn't you tell me that you knew about Eric?"

Michelle's eyes could not hold back the tears.

"I wanted to tell you, Dessie," she replied. "I swear I wanted…"

Once again, Dereé cut her off.

"I don't want to hear any more, Micki. All I know is my life is upside down, and I have to put it back together."

Dereé adjusted her seatbelt, while Michelle kept her eyes on the road.

"I found out about Eric from Chance," Dereé continued.

Michelle's body tensed up and she gripped the steering wheel at the mention of Chance's name. Dereé was too consumed with her thoughts to notice.

She placed one hand in the other and fiddled with her fingers as she continued. "I called Chance at his office the day after you and I talked about what he could possibly have on Eric. He arranged to meet me in Fairmont Park near the creek. He sounded a little different when I spoke to him, but he agreed to meet me."

Dereé looked up and paused for a moment before telling her friend about the night that changed her view of her husband.

"I drove to our appointed spot and waited in my car. It was like torture waiting for Chance to arrive. After about thirty minutes of waiting, I started to panic and began calling his cell phone back to back, but he never answered."

In a shaky voice, Michelle asked, "What do you mean? I thought you said he told you about Eric?"

Dereseé turned and looked at Michelle. She realized they had been driving for about twenty minutes and was now going in the opposite direction of her home. Before she answered Michelle's question, she addressed the fact that she was concerned about where they were going.

"Michelle, where are we going? We're nowhere near my house. Not that I even want to see Eric besides in a coffin."

"I have to show you something and you don't need to be home alone right now anyway," Michelle told her.

Michelle felt nervous about Dereseé's story and having to come clean about what happened to Eric.

"I hope it's nothing worse than what I've already been through tonight!" Dereseé faced Michelle as she continued. "Like I was saying…Chance didn't answer his phone, but he showed up about twenty minutes later, now almost an hour late. He swerved in the parking spot. I exited my car and stood behind his car with my arms crossed. He finally got out and headed toward me while rubbing the back of his head. He stopped in front of me and just stared at me. When I asked why he was late, he said:

"Dereseé, I need you to just listen. My reason for being late is not important. I have something on Eric that you will not believe. I just need you to have an open mind. It started about four months ago when I first started having him tailed."

Chance leaned on the car for support and pulled Dereseé close to him.

"I was on business at the Hilton Hotel in New Jersey, when I thought I saw Eric. I followed him up on the adjacent elevator hoping to just catch a glimpse of you. When I turned the corner, my eyes bugged out of my head. I saw him and two people going into a hotel suite pawing at each other."

Desereé stopped telling the story. Her head sunk into the palms of her hands, and the tears flowed from all the hurt and lies she had endured. Michelle pulled into a parking spot and consoled her friend by hugging her tightly. She wiped her eyes and refused to let any more tears invade her pretty brown pupils. Desereé took a deep breath and then continued to tell Michelle about that night with Chance.

"I began to yell at him and tell him that he was mistaken...not two women at once. Chance grabbed my hands as he continued to take me on the sick journey Eric had traveled. He reached in his back pocket, pulled out a torn picture, and told me:

"Dessie, I wish I could tell you that he had two women or that it just happened once, but the truth is it happened several times a week per my private investigator.

"He paused, almost hesitant to continue the story. I pounded on his chest and began to cry. Just as I snatched the photo out of his hand, he said what it revealed..."

"It was a man and a woman with a jeweled mask on, and they..."

"I stopped him in mid-sentence and started pushing and punching on him. I screamed louder and louder. I demanded that he give me any other pictures he had, and he told me that he didn't have them. He backed up as he tried to explain they were stolen. The angrier I got, the harder I hit him...until his foot hit a rock and he went flying backward. He fell and his head landed on a tree stump. I ran over to the passenger side of his car and climbed in, searching for more evidence. I found nothing but an empty folder with pieces of photos. I took off and left him there. I'm horrible! He could be dead. How could I do that to him, when he was only trying to help me?"

Michelle's heart pounded uncontrollably. She knew her earlier fight with Chance had a lot to do with him being unstable during their struggle.

"You didn't mean to hurt him, Dessie. Calm down. I'm sure he's ok," Michelle said, trying to console her.

Michelle hoped what she had told Dereseé was the truth. She really hoped he was okay. She was quickly turning into a snake in the grass that held many secrets from her friend.

Michelle reached out to Desereé, took hold of her hands, and told her, "Dessie, I have to show you something, but I need you to be prepared for this. I've done something for you that I hope you understand."

Desereé moved to the edge of her seat and listened closely.

*****

Sanai drove like she wasn't trying to live through the night. She disregarded several red lights and stop signs. Layla had to keep up, taking chances with her life in order to catch up to her friend. She knew Sanai needed her, and that was enough reason for her to keep up the chase.

Just two blocks from her home set in Willow Grove, Pennsylvania, where trees lined the streets and flowers were plenty, Sanai ran the light as she turned the corner on two wheels like the Duke of Hazzard. As she approached the next corner, Layla could see her racing for the light. Sanai swerved to avoid hitting a parked car and clipped a street pole, but she kept going. Sanai made a sharp left into her smooth-paved driveway.

Sanai jumped out of her car, leaving the door open as she ran up her front porch steps trying to get inside of the house quickly. She just wanted to be alone and evaporate into thin air. She hated herself for being so stupid and actually starting to fall for Eric. Now she had been served a death sentence. All of her promiscuous ways and evil secret had finally caught up with her, and karma was staring her in the face.

She could hear a car pulling up in her driveway as she fell in her front door. Sanai lay on the floor in her foyer sobbing uncontrollably.

"My fucking life is over! I never thought it would end like this! I'm ruined, " she yelled in between sobs.

Layla ran through the door, tripping over Sanai's limp body as she lay screaming various random statements.

"Sanai, please calm down. It will be okay. I just know it will. It has to be."

Layla allowed her feelings to match Sanai's emotions as she embraced her tightly…so close that she could feel her heart beat. Even after one of her ugly secrets had been exposed Layla still loved Sanai.

Sanai had a brief flashback and became enraged. She pushed Layla off of her, and using her hands and bottom, she scooted away from her. Layla went tumbling backward.

"You're sick, I tell you," Sanai snarled. "Get your damn hands off of me. I read what you wrote in that sick diary of yours. I cringed as I read page after page of what you wanted to do to me and me to you. It will never happen! Never!"

Surprised by Sanai's switch in emotions, Layla's face mirrored surprise and shock.

"What the hell is wrong with you? You treat me like shit! All I wanted was to be with you. How can you say those horrible things to me? Sanai, you can't mean what you're saying. I know you're just upset right now. You don't mean it. You can't. The way you performed with me, I know it was real."

Sanai sat straight up. "Are you retarded, bitch? I like men. It was an experimental thing. I'm fucking dying, and you're still on this shit? Get out now! Get out! Just go! You want to possess me like your brother did."

Layla stood to her feet at the mention of her brother King. "Sanai, take that shit back. You know he loved you and wanted nothing but the best for you. How could you say that about him?"

Sanai began to laugh hysterically; she had really lost it. "Are you serious?" Sanai said, standing up to match Layla's stance. "I think it's time for me to tell you about your slimy-ass brother whom did nothing but take my heart and killed my soul. I died the day I found him screwing my lowlife cousin two days before our anniversary. So, screw you and him. I blame him for everything, even my HIV status."

Layla lunged forward as Sanai delivered more verbal blows. She slapped Sanai so hard that she split her lip and sent her spinning counterclockwise. Layla jumped back to avoid contact with Sanai's infected blood.

"So I guess you were fronting all of these years, pretending to be sharing in my sorrow over my brother's death. You know what, Sanai? Maybe the other girls are right about you being rotten to the core. You can stay here and rot for all I care."

Layla turned to walk away, but the words Sanai uttered next would send Layla into a complete rage.

"You think I care about you leaving? I could care less. I'm prepared to die alone. Your brother made sure I was cold and callous. That's why I sent him to meet his maker early. It felt good when I heard the gunshots, just as I planned. He slumped over me, and I saw him take his last breath…needing me …wanting me to get him help. I rejoiced in his pain, as it matched the pain he caused me."

Layla ran full speed and body slammed Sanai. They both landed in the doorway of Sanai's dining room. Layla screamed from the pit of her belly as she wrapped her hands around Sanai's neck.

"You bitch! You bitch!" Layla continued to cry over and over while banging Sanai's head on the floor.

Sanai felt her body losing oxygen fast. She became dizzy as she reached at the air while looking far off into the distance, her eyes unable to focus.

"To actually think I felt remorse for orchestrating your demise," Sanai murmured.

She could see a fuzzy male figure approaching her, which she assumed to be a vision of King. The image got closer, and then Sanai heard a loud thump before her eyes closed.

*****

Desereé and Michelle approached the door. Desereé fought back the tears. She had mixed feelings about what she was about to see behind the door. As they got close enough to see the numbers on the door, they saw the Do Not Disturb sign still hanging where Michelle left it. The pair stood hand in hand as Michelle reached her left hand out to place the key in the slot. The green light on the door lit up, and Desereé turned the handle.

As they stepped inside of the suite, the sight was alarming. Michelle quickly searched for her phone. Desereé walked toward the bedroom and began to scream. Michelle stepped over the trash and broken lamp to run to her rescue. When she turned the corner, Michelle dropped to her knees. The bedroom was trashed just like the living room area, but Eric was nowhere to be found.

Michelle quickly called the hospital to be sure Trevor was still in a locked down unit. She felt horrible that she had disclosed Trevor's status to Eric, and now, he was in fact not dead but on the loose.

*****

Groggy and half-dressed, Eric struggled down the back stairs of the hotel. The news that Michelle had told him was unbelievable. He had millions of thoughts running through his mind. His biggest regret was having unprotected sex with Sanai and Trevor. He hated both of them, and they were going to pay.

He located his car in the parking lot and stumbled to the driver's door. He struggled to focus getting his key in the door. Once inside, he started the car and rolled down all of his windows, taking deep breaths to remain conscience. After about ten minutes, he drove off, heading for reciprocity.

*****

Now unsure of Eric's emotional state, Dereseé paced the hotel room, while Michelle called the hospital to be sure Eric had not showed up there to see Trevor. Dereseé and Michelle knew Eric wanted both of his lovers to pay for his terrible fate to come soon. Michelle was now added to his list and may soon feel his wrath, also.

Dereseé turned to Michelle and said, "Micki, I think I know where he went."

Then, in unison, they both said, "Sanai!"

The pair took off running for the door. Although they hated Sanai with a passion, all of the ownership was not her own, and Layla did not deserve to get caught up in their mess. Michelle and Dereseé ran to the elevator and headed to stop Eric on his quest for revenge.

Sanai

Beginning Of The End

Sanai's house had become a torture chamber and deathtrap. All the curtains in the home remain closed, and now the front door was closed and locked. Sanai awoke from her forced slumber with a banging headache. She struggled to regain her eyesight and attempted to get up to explore her surroundings. She couldn't move far because her hands and feet were tied to her dining room chair situated in the center of the room.

"Layla! Layla…what are you doing?" Sanai began to yell, but her calls went unanswered.

She attempted to turn herself around and fell over, landing on her side. Staring at Layla's limp body in the corner of the dining room, Sanai let out a big scream. Just then, she felt her chair being lifted from the floor. Now concerned about what was going on, Sanai began to scream. She could hear the footsteps now walking away toward her kitchen.

"Help! Help!" she yelled. Her newfound will to live took over her body. "Eric, please don't do this to me. What are you doing? I didn't know. I swear I didn't know."

Sanai pleaded for her life. She didn't know what was about to happen. All she knew was that Layla was possibly dead, and she was not too far behind her. She tried to reason with him again.

"Eric, you can live long with HIV. I swear killing me won't solve anything."

Still, the mysterious guest said nothing; they just moved about running water and gathering things. Sanai turned her body, attempting to catch a glimpse of her captor.

Feeling defeated, Sanai hung her head low, still unable to move her arms and legs. She heard footsteps coming toward her. Frightened but curious, she lifted her head and attempted to focus her eyes on the image approaching. What appeared to be a large male figure walked toward her carrying glass serving tray that had a blue cocktail in a martini glass sitting on it. Her neck was sore, and her head pounded as she struggled to keep her head up. Her body began to shake as the figure came in view. Now face to face and staring her in the eyes, the man evoked fear from deep in her belly.

"Noooooooo! Help! Help!" Sanai yelled. "It can't be. What happened to you?"

The man stood tall and muscular with a gruesome scar on his face that separated his nose and cheekbone. "It's me in the flesh, baby. What, did you think I was gone forever? Oh...does my scar offend you? I owe this all to you. I have a nice cocktail for you to take the edge off. I know how you love your martinis.

I put something special in it just for you. Don't worry, you'll be able to view the show, but your movement will be restricted."

Sanai could see a torture kit inside of a black velvet case that lay beside the cocktail. She started to swing her head around wildly, attempting to knock the drink off of the tray. She waited until the drink was close enough and hit it off of the tray with her forehead. As the blue deadly cocktail went crashing to the floor, Sanai felt a sharp pain on her cheek from a backhand slap.

"Bitch, now you will endure this torture all by yourself."

Sanai mustered up enough strength to address her attacker.

"Corey, I'm sorry," she whispered. "What have I done to you? What happened to your face?"

At one time, many had desired Corey, but now he was hideous.

"Oh, this old scar? I got this up state while doing time for the crime you set me up on. Despite your attempts to get me booked for King's murder, the prosecutor couldn't produce the weapon. Therefore, I couldn't be charged with murder-one. They did find another crime to pin on me and lock me in that animal cage for a while. So, here I am twelve years later ready to do what I dreamed about nightly for over a decade."

Sanai's eyes widened as Corey went on about how he knew she was the anonymous informant regarding who killed King. Crying, she knew she wouldn't make it out of this alive. Corey continued to talk while unwrapping his torture tools.

"Don't cry now. I've seen you come and go without a care in the world for the past few months. You met your boyfriend for dinner and kicked it with your girls with no compassion for the person who killed for you. You didn't even send a card or answer my calls when I attempted to reach out to you the first five years I was away. For that, you will pay with your life."

Corey paced back and forth in front of Sanai, contemplating his first form of revenge. Coming to a decision, he turned on his jigsaw. Sanai began to yell again, not wanting to feel the pain she was about to endure. Once obsessed with Sanai and willing to do anything for her, Corey now stared down at her feeling nothing as he drilled his handy tool into her thigh. Blood squirted everywhere as Sanai yelled.

"Ohhhhh...owwww! Please stop, Corey!"

He walked around her chair and stopped on the other side of her. "This is for the long nights in prison when I felt like I had no legs. No matter how hard I tried, I was stuck."

Corey brought the jigsaw down on her left thigh. Sanai began to thrust forward as if she were going to vomit. He smiled, his large scar seeming to separate his face. He then stepped to the side and leaned in close to Sanai. His lips touched her earlobe.

"Listen to me closely. I have lots more to do to you. You may want to breathe before you pass out. Don't worry, though. I'll bring you back."

Corey walked over to his tools and picked up a scalpel, then a meat tenderizer. He returned to Sanai with the scalpel and alcohol in his hands. He then proceeded to make deep incisions in both of her forearms and pour alcohol over the wounds.

"Just kill me please!" Sanai cried in agony.

Corey's anger grew as she yelled at him. He raised his right hand holding the scalpel and jammed the instrument into her right shoulder. Sanai's body trembled, and her eyes rolled in the back of her head. When Corey leaned in to see if she was breathing, he was met with a swift, hard blow to the back of his head.

A weak Layla delivered blow after blow, while yelling, "You killed my brother! Die! Die! Die!" She continued hitting him until he wasn't moving.

Layla stepped back, dropped the meat tenderizer, and lurched to the front door, still foggy from the unconscious slumber she awoke from. With tears flowing and not believing how wrong her night had gone, she unlocked the door so she could head home. As she opened the front door, Michelle and Deseree were running up on the porch.

Seeing blood all over Layla's arms and shirt, Michelle pushed past her and headed for the back. As she entered the dining room, she saw a man, who was clearly not Eric, lying on the floor nonresponsive and losing a lot of blood. Her eyes grew wide in fear. She was certain Eric was there. Now, she had to think of a quick way to get out of the mess she'd gotten herself into.

Seeing Sanai's limp body tied up and hunched over, Michelle leaned down and checked for a pulse, but found nothing. Judging by the gruesome sight of the room, she concluded the wounds Sanai sustained from the torture sent her into shock. She wrestled with her oath as a doctor and her loyalty to Deseree. As much as Michelle wanted to leave Sanai lying there after the drama she caused, she just couldn't walk away. This was what Michelle took pride in, holding people's lives in the palm of her hand. Besides, with Eric missing, she had to do her best not to buckle under the pressure and draw attention to herself. For the first time, she was scared and had no clue how to bring an end to this drama. So, until she was able to solve the mystery of Eric's missing body, she had to remain cool.

Michelle used the scalpel on the floor to cut Sanai's restraints. She yelled to Dereeé, who stood in disbelief as she looked around at the scene like she was watching an episode of *CSI*.

"Call 9-1-1!" Michelle yelled with urgency, then laid Sanai on the floor and began CPR.

Dereeé snapped out of her trance and ran to the kitchen to get the cordless phone that sat on a counter by the entrance. She dialed the numbers nervously, clicked on the speakerphone, and held it up to Michelle's face so she could clearly communicate with the operator. A woman answered the call. She had a high-pitched, nasal-sounding voice. The tempo of her voice suggested she operated on only two modes, slow and slower.

"9-1-1…what's your emergency?" the woman said.

"This is Dr. Michelle Jacobs," Michelle replied. "I need an ambulance now. I have D.O.A.-African-American male about 6'2", 225 pounds. There is evidence of blunt force trauma to the head. I also have an African-American female; 5'10", 145 pounds with multiple lacerations from some kind of power saw. She is not breathing. I'm currently performing CPR."

The woman answered slowly as if this was a normal occurrence. "Okay, we'll dispatch a unit immediately."

Michelle thought, *I hope they come faster than you sound.*

Michelle provided the address to the woman, who dispatched a unit to Sanai's house. In reality, Michelle really wanted Sanai to die for what she'd done to Dereseé, but she had to put those thoughts aside and do her job.

A few moments later, sounds of people walking heavily toward the dining room could be heard. Two EMT's and the coroner entered the dining room. One of the EMT's froze at the sight. *Oh my God!* she thought to herself as she scanned the scene. She witnessed a dead body and another victim fighting for her life in a pool of her own blood. Normally, she would have jumped in without thought and just did her job, but there was something about this she found to be very eerie.

Suddenly, a male voice called out, "Jackson, call this in! She's lost a lot of blood. We've got to get her to the emergency room…STAT!"

The EMT's continued working on Sanai after loading her almost lifeless body into the ambulance and speeding off.

The police also responded to the call and arrived just a few minutes after. They sealed off the crime scene with police tape as they began their investigation. Michelle calmly spoke to the police officer, explaining what happened from the point they entered the house. After giving the officer her version of the account, she looked at Dereseé, who stood in the corner of the room on the verge of falling apart. Her body was shaking as tears welled up in her eyes. Seeing this, Michelle kindly excused herself, grabbed Dereseé by the hand, and quickly escorted her outside to the car.

"Micki, I can't believe this is happening."

Michelle, trying to be as comforting as possible without letting on that she was also scared shitless, said, "Look, you have got to try and keep it together."

"How can I? Our hands are stained with blood. What's worse is that my husband, who you supposedly left for dead, is somewhere out there and we don't know where! So, I'm sorry if I'm a little scared for my life right now," Dereseé told her, trembling with fear.

"You think I don't know that?" Michelle's annoyance with Dereseé caused her voice to rise slightly. She stepped back and took a deep breath before continuing. "Look, let's just go to the hospital and find out what's going on with Sanai. Then, we'll go from there. Okay?"

The two got into Michelle's car. This was heat neither one of them wanted. From the looks of it, they were clueless as to how to get out of the kitchen. The ugly truth was they were in too deep. They had to see this through or they would perish.

*****

The cleaning lady walked in and out of the hotel rooms doing her usual routine of cleaning up the messes that guests often made during their stay. She was a short, full-figured Puerto Rican woman, roughly in her mid-fifties and who didn't speak much English. Despite the lack of care the guests showed when it came to the upkeep of the room, she took pride in going in and creating order out of chaos.

With her earbuds in her ear, she sang to the tunes blasting from her iPod that she got as a birthday present from her children. Although she didn't know how to use it very well, she clearly knew how to push play and crank up the volume, especially when her favorite songs came on. As the sounds of

Reggaton Latino filled her ears, she danced around her cart and headed to her next room. She took her key and unlocked the room. She stood frozen at the front door. She thought her eyes were playing tricks on her.

She turned down her music and whispered, "Ay dios' mio!" She walked slowly into the room unsure of what she would find. Growing annoyed, she said, "Esto no tiene sentido! ¿Cómo podría alguien esta sala como esta de la basura?"

She turned her music back up and proceeded to change the sheets on the bed. As she pulled them off the bed, she noticed something that looked like candy and a piece of paper. She picked them up with her gloved hand and looked at them closely. She realized what she held in her hand was not candy but some kind of pill. She opened the piece of paper and began to attempt to read what it said. Unfortunately, she could only translate a few words. What she was able to translate was, *I couldn't bear living.*

As she held the sheet from the bed in her hand, she noticed streaks of blood. The cleaning lady dropped everything, screamed frantically, and ran out of the room straight to the manager's office.

When the lady arrived in the hotel's lobby, she screamed for the manager. She didn't realize guests were waiting to check in. At that point, she didn't care.

The manager ran out of his office in horror, not because of the lady's screams but because he didn't want to alarm the guests. He quickly attempted to diffuse the situation by pulling the hysterical woman into his office.

"Luz, what is going on?" he whispered.

Gasping for air, Luz tried to calm down. Between each deep breath, she said, "Die! Room! Someone die!"

"What do you mean someone die?"

Forgetting that the manager did not speak an ounce of Spanish, she began telling her story. The words poured out so fast she could barely catch her breath.

"Voy a 105 como siempre. Abro la puerta. Era totalmente destrozado. Sillas, Mesas y televisión fueron entregados y la cama estaba en ruinas. Había papel higiénico y basura por todas partes. Cuando fui a cambiar las hojas, me encontré con pastillas y una carta que decía 'Yo no podía tener vida'. Luego encontré sangre en las hojas. ¡Dios mío! No puedo creerlo. Alguien morir."

(Translation: "I go into 105, as usual. I open the door. It was completely trashed. Chairs, tables, and television were turned over, and the bed was in shambles. There was toilet paper and trash everywhere. When I went to change the sheets, I found pills and a letter that said, 'I couldn't bear living'. Then I found blood on the sheets. Oh my God! I can't believe it. Someone die.")

The manager tried hard to stop her because he didn't understand what Luz was trying to say. He called for another member of the cleaning staff to come in to translate. As he listened, his face became pale. Never in all his years of working at the hotel had he ever encountered anything like this on his watch. He reached for the phone and immediately called the police, who arrived in record time.

They walked into the manager's office to find the manager, Luz, and her translator seated with looks of shock on their faces. The police took Luz's statement and then went to the scene of the crime as the rest followed. Through the police tape, detectives and forensics officers from the crime lab rushed in with an arsenal of gadgets needed to compile evidence. They inspected every inch of the room, leaving no stone unturned. They took samples of blood from the fibers in the sheet, bagged up the pills and note, and then dusted for prints.

As they continued their investigation, a detective yelled, "Hey, come take a look at this."

Two of his colleagues rushed over to see what the officer was looking at.

"We have a strand of hair, ladies and gentlemen. Get me DNA analysis on this," the detective said with authority.

An officer carefully collected the sample of hair, bagged it as evidence, and rushed off.

One of the female officers on the scene walked up to the detective who was deep in thought. He was awakened by her voice.

"Hey, sir…what's your take on this?"

The detective gave her a cross look as he rubbed his head.

"Something doesn't smell right about this. A suicide with a missing body? I'm going to get to the bottom of this one way or another."

Layla

Lethal Cocktale

Layla swerved in and out of traffic on the expressway. Surprisingly, she made it home without getting into an accident and or getting pulled over. After pulling up in her driveway, she sat in her car and cried. The guilt set in that she didn't listen to her husband and went out anyway. Not only that, but she also was about to walk in with another man's blood on her clothes. She didn't know where to begin with Darren, but an explanation was needed.

She wiped her tears away and got herself together to walk inside their home. As she entered, she spotted the kitchen light on and walked into the kitchen, heading straight for the sink to wash away the blood. Darren crept in and stood behind her. He startled her as he spoke.

"So you went out anyway?"

Layla jumped before she turned around. At the sight of blood, Darren's whole demeanor changed. He wanted to know what transpired for her to be covered in blood.

"Layla, what's wrong? Talk to me," he said, while checking her to see if she had any injuries.

In and out of shock, Layla began crying again.

"Layla, I have no time for tears. Snap out of it and tell me what happened."

She sniffled and garnered the strength to speak about the events that took place earlier that evening.

"Well, the night was going great. We were having drinks, but it all just took a turn for the worse. I ended up finding out my best friend was sleeping with another one of my friend's husband. They started fighting; Sanai and I had a fight and argument. I ended up at her house, and then it gets fuzzy for me. All I remember is waking up dazed and confused but spotting Corey. And when I say Corey, it's the Corey that had something to do with murdering King. I saw him standing over Sanai with blood everywhere, and I clocked him over the head a couple of times. I think I might have killed him."

Layla's lips trembled as tears welled up in her eyes.

"And my best friend might be dead, too. I don't know, but while running out the house, Dereseé and Michelle were on their way in. I didn't even stop. I just wanted to get home to you," Layla concluded as she broke down in tears again. This time, her body began to break down, as well.

Darren caught his wife before she could hit the floor. He was furious with her, but deep down, he knew this was not the time to chastise her. He scooped her up, carried her into the living room, and placed her on the couch. He then went into her purse, pulled out her phone, and began calling her friends. First call was to Sanai, but her phone went straight to voicemail. He called the next person on his mind, which was Dereseé.

"Layla, where are you?" Dereseé answered.

"This is Darren. Look, Layla is hysterical and needs medical attention. I'm taking her to a hospital."

"Darren, we're on our way to Abington Hospital. Bring her here."

"Okay, we're on our way," he said, then hung up.

Darren was in a panic, but he knew Abington Hospital was just a short distance from their Jenkintown residence.

After scooping up Layla, they were out the door and on their way to the hospital.

Darren drove through traffic like a Nascar racer. While driving, he tried to keep his eyes on the road and at the same time keep a close eye on his wife. Nodding in and out, Layla looked like a dope fiend who had their fix.

"Layla, wake up, babe," Darren said as he raised her head up by placing his free hand under her chin.

As he lifted her head, he spotted the wound on the side of her head. That's when he put the pedal to the metal and began driving even faster. Darren finally made it to the emergency entrance and double-parked in front. Hopping out, he yelled for help. He caught the attention of two male workers who were on a smoke break. Both males dropped their cigarettes and began helping him immediately.

"Sir, what's your emergency?" asked the one dark-skinned male.

"It's my wife; she has a head injury. She might be suffering from blunt trauma. She's going in and out of consciousness."

After speaking to the man, Darren checked on Layla who was lying in the passenger seat, while the other gentleman ran into the hospital to get a stretcher. The man who stayed to help pulled out a mini flashlight and flashed the light in her eyes. Layla's eyes rolled around her sockets as he checked her state of consciousness.

"She's stable but might be in a state of shock from the wound. How did she receive this injury?" the man inquired.

For the moment, Darren skipped over answering that question.

"Look, I can answer that later. I know you have protocol, but fuck that right now. My wife needs medical attention."

After Darren finished speaking, the other worker exited the sliding doors with the hospital bed on wheels. They picked her up out of the car, placed her on the bed, and wheeled her inside.

While following them, Darren whispered in her ear, "Be strong, babe. I got you help."

Once the medical personnel took her in the back to attend to her needs, Darren went straight to the front desk to meet with the attendant.

"We're going to need you to fill out this paperwork for insurance purposes," the middle-aged lady told him as she pulled out the paperwork secured to a clipboard.

Darren ran out to the car and got her purse that held all the information he needed to fill out the paperwork. Once back in the waiting room, he filled out the papers, handed them to the front desk clerk, and was told to wait patiently in the waiting room. While waiting, he paced back and forth, unable to sit down to await the status on his wife. He pulled out her phone and called Sanai, whose phone went straight to voicemail again. Just as he was about to call Desereé, the doctor walked out to give him an update.

"Is there a Mr. Smith in the room?"

Darren approached the doctor to acknowledge himself.

"Yes, that would be me. How's my wife?" Darren asked nervously.

"I'm Dr. Arenas, and she will be fine, sir. She's just suffering from a minor head injury. We patched her up. She just needs to get some rest. We normally don't recommend that for a head wound, but her vitals are fine and we have nurses checking on her periodically. Do you know how she sustained the injury to her head, sir?"

"All I can tell you is that she was out with friends and ended up at one of her friend's house. That's where it all took place."

"Should we notify the authorities?" Dr. Arenas asked.

"Yes. I would like to get to the bottom of this," Darren demanded.

The doctor made his way to the front desk and asked the clerk to dial 911 immediately. Then he walked back over to where Darren was standing.

"Sir, give her about another thirty minutes, and when the cops arrive, we should get her stabilized so they can make a full report."

191

"Okay. Thanks, doc," Darren said as he shook the doctor's hand.

Darren's nervousness was subsided by the doctor's words that his wife would be okay. He sat down and waited the arrival of the cops.

Michelle and Deserȩ́e arrived at Abington Hospital Emergency Department. Deserȩ́e walked around looking like a lost puppy trying to find her owner. Michelle felt right at home. She was in her element.

Michelle looked at the board, and to her surprise, not only was Sanai's name posted but Layla's, as well. With Deserȩ́e waiting in the lobby, Sanai and Layla laid up in the emergency room, Chance possibly dead, Trevor in the psych ward, and Eric nowhere to be found, she knew a storm was brewing. This time, she didn't know how to calm it. Nevertheless, she went right to work searching for answers.

*****

Forty minutes later, two officers arrived and went straight to the front desk. Due to there being a couple of people in the lobby, Darren didn't know they were there for him until he saw the lady pointing in his direction. He stood up as they approached him. Just then, he heard Dr. Arenas' name being called over the hospital's PA system. Once they were in his presence, one officer who looked like he was on a donut diet spoke up.

"Hello, I'm Officer Mallory, and this is my partner Officer Jordan."

They shook Darren's hand as Darren observed that they looked like a before and after Weight Watchers picture. Officer Mallory pulled out a notepad and pen from his chest area.

"Okay, sir, we're going to start the report. Could you go over what took place?"

"Can we wait for the doctor? He told me that he wants you guys to be able to talk to my wife."

"So you don't know what happened?" Officer Mallory asked.

"Vaguely. I wasn't present with my wife at the time. But, I would rather let her tell it since she's the one who was there," Darren said as he folded his arms and waited for the arrival of Dr. Arenas.

The double doors of the emergency room opened up as the doctor walked into the waiting area. Dr. Arenas introduced himself to the officers cordially and shook their hands.

"Listen, good news. She's actually awake but a little shaky. Now, if everybody would follow me, I will lead the way."

When they arrived, Layla was sitting on the edge of the bed putting her pants on, her head wrapped up like a mummy. Darren quickly ran in to plant a kiss on his wife's lips.

"Hey, babe, how you feel?

Layla smiled, but her smile quickly faded as she placed both hands on the side of her head.

"Darren, don't speak so loudly. I have a migraine."

"Sorry, babe. The cops are here, and they're ready to get a statement. Are you ready to talk?"

"Yes, Darren, damn. Stop treating me like I just got off the small yellow bus."

Darren backed off, but he knew since she cracked a small joke that she was okay. Officer stepped up from the background with his notepad and pen in hand.

"So can you walk us through the events that led to your injury, ma'am?"

Layla inhaled, preparing to do what she knew she had to do. Until this moment, she was viewed as a supporting actress only. This was her time to shine.

"Yes, bear with me. It's a little choppy, but I think I can manage to tie the pieces together," Layla said, then took another deep breath and let it out as tears welled up in her eyes.

"Officer, it all started when me and three other friends, Sanai, Michelle and Dereseé, were having cocktails as we've done every month for the past three years. Tonight was a little different as far as location. We usually meet at the Rum Bar, but we changed to Positano Coast Lounge for some new scenery. The drinks were plentiful and atmosphere lively, but one thing led to another. Arguments began and secrets started flying out of the closet. I remember a couple of fights took place. It was horrible."

Pulled in by the story, the officers grabbed a seat and attempted to slow things down.

"Ma'am, can you please be more specific? What were the arguments over? Who was at the helm of them? And I need to know the secrets you are referring to. It may be a motive of some kind."

Layla had not taken acting classes, but she was dead-on playing the victim in this scenario. The officers had fallen face first in her trap. She held her head in her hands and began to sob.

Hugging her, Darren said, "Babe, if it's too much, we can do this some other day."

Not knowing that he, too, was a voyeur to the Layla's show, Darren attempted to aid her. Layla lifted her head from the palms of her hands and looked him in his eyes.

"No, babe, I have to do this, even though it will hurt."

She continued with her story while the two police officers acted as stenographers.

"Okay, Michelle was a little late, and when she arrived, all hell broke loose. Michelle came in waving papers and pictures of Sanai sleeping with Deseree's husband, Eric. Michelle attacked Sanai and…"

Layla began to gasp for air and hold her chest as she hyperventilated. The doctor ran to her side and encouraged Layla to take deep breaths. While rubbing her leg, Darren assisted the doctor in trying to calm her. As her breathing slowed down, the room was silent. The officers anticipated hearing what could have been so awful to send her into a mini panic attack. She regained control of her breathing and continued.

"…gave her a paper with Eric and his gay lover Trevor's HIV test results, which were positive."

Layla's last words caused her to tear up as her mouth trembled. Darren wrapped his arms around his wife to console her. Officer Jordan reached over and grabbed some tissue for her. The tears she cried were real this time, but her reasons for them were all too different. She knew her final "cocktale" would separate the group forever. She had to say goodbye to a friend who she had loved for over fifteen years, and now knowing the truth, she truly mourned her brother's death. Layla took another deep breath after wiping away the tears.

"After the fights, my friend Sanai was destroyed, and Dereseé was sick with grief about the HIV news. She ran off and Sanai abruptly left to go to her house. I followed her to be sure she was safe and not going to do anything crazy. After arriving at Sanai's house, I consoled her, and we talked about how she possibly may not have HIV.

"We received a call from Michelle saying she was going to meet up with us there to apologize for what took place. So, we are there and she arrived, knocking on the door. When I opened the door to let her in, a big male was with her. I began to scream at her, and all I remember from there is waking up and watching Michelle repeatedly hit him over the head with a blunt object. When I saw my best friend lying in blood, I panicked, got up, ran out of there, and hopped in my car. In my rearview mirror, I could see Michelle coming behind me. So, I put my foot on the gas and sped off."

There was a brief pause after those words escaped her mouth. Then she let out a loud scream.

"My best friend in the world was helpless, Darren!"

Layla broke down in tears again. She wanted to be sure they viewed her as the helpless friend who got caught up in a lover's crossfire. Her feelings about Sanai were once true, but now, they were replaced with detest and hatred. Sanai had taken her brother from her and stolen fifteen years of her life. She would have to pay for that. Michelle had always been arrogant and had an above-the-law attitude. She treated Layla like an airhead that followed Sanai around. Layla decided she would pay the ultimate price.

Officer Mallory, who was jotting down all the details of her accounts, stopped writing and watched as everybody waited for Layla to get herself together.

"Do you have a last name for those two ladies you mentioned?"

Before speaking, Layla wiped her nose as fluids began to seep out.

"Yes, I do. Sanai Jackson and Michelle Martin."

Dr. Arenas stepped up when he heard the name Michelle Martin. With a look of concern on his face, he interrupted her story.

"Wait. Do you mean Dr. Michelle Jacobs?"

"Yes. As a matter of fact, she works here," Layla replied, looking in the direction of Dr. Arenas, who had a look of shock on his face.

Darren shook the officers' hands and then turned to tend to his wife.

Dr. Arenas left the room and went to the nurse's hub on the floor to have Michelle located. He could still see the two officers in his view as he passed the room where Layla remained. He was desperate to find his colleague/friend to find out if the young woman's statement could be true before the police found her. She was not only being accused of murder, but also one of the worse things a doctor could do—sharing a patient's health information. She would definitely lose her license and do jail time if found guilty.

The officers conversed in a whisper before leaving the room.

Leaning in, Mallory whispered, "I heard a call for the address that the vic gave us, and it was for an unresponsive female and D.O.A. male vic. I think we have something here."

As they stepped into the hallway, the partners agreed to call the station. They spotted Dr. Arenas heading to the south wing of the ER. Being the leader of the pair, Mallory called the station and confirmed what he had already thought. Aftere his call he turned to his partner and said, "The person on the scene at Saina's house had identified herself as a Dr. Martin". Officer Jordan thanked Layla for her cooperation and the pair hurried to begin their investigation.

*****

Michelle and Deseree conversed in the hallway as they attempted to put together the pieces of the horrible evening. Still in shock, Deseree wrapped a heated blanket around her and continued to talk things through with Michelle. Now cleaned up and dressed in scrubs, Michelle continued to assure Deseree that everything was going to be all right. They stood just feet away from the room where Sanai lay being worked on as the doctors attempted to get her stable enough for surgery.

Michelle's mouth moved with confidence and assurance, but her mind was on the verge of breakdown. She was consumed with the loose end called Eric that she thought she had tied up.

Where could his body be? she thought to herself. *Someone is playing tricks on me. Maybe it's Chance, or maybe he's not dead and he's at the police station right now planning my fall.*

As Desereé continued to talk, sounding more like background noise, Michelle was jarred from her thoughts when the loud speaker throughout the emergency room called a code for Sanai's room. Michelle instructed Desereé to go to the waiting room and then turned to get involved in the action. As she ran to Sanai's room, she could see her colleague Dr. Arenas headed her way. When she reached the door of Sanai's room, she was told she could not assist in the emergency.

Upon reaching a now annoyed Michelle, Dr. Arenas told her, "Dr. Martin, I need a word with you."

Michelle had always respected Dr. Arenas and knew he had lots of power in the hospital. She calmed down and stepped aside with him.

"I have to talk to you about a development I was just informed of."

Michelle's eyes widened. She had many secrets from being a high-paid call girl, interfering with patient information, to murder and deception. She didn't know what he was speaking of but feared the worse.

As they stood outside of Sanai's room, she saw two police officers coming down the hallway holding a piece of paper and pointing in her direction. Her mouth dried up and her ears began to ring. Her fate was unknown. The two officers approached her and Dr. Arenas. Officer Mallory looked at the photo he had retrieved from the nurse's hub and then looked at her.

"Michelle Martin, we need to speak with you down at the station."

Just then, Michelle became undone. "Speak to me about what? I save lives. Do you know who I am? Do you?" She waved her arms in the air. "You have nothing on me. Nothing, I tell you."

Not sure what had gone wrong, Deseree ran to her friend's side and advised her to exercise her Fifth Amendment rights. Michelle was too far gone, though. She yelled obscenities at the cops and threatened to have them handled for embarrassing her in her "house". The casual trip to the station had quickly turned ugly. Michelle was being placed under arrest. Officer Jordan grabbed her right hand, turned her to face the wall, and handcuffed her.

"You have the right to remain silent. You have the right to an attorney…" he said, reading her the Miranda Rights.

Michelle wiggled and yelled over him, "Fuck you and your rights! I'm the closest to God. You're gonna see. I fix things. That's what I do. Take these damn cuff off of me."

Deseree broke down; her rock was coming unglued before her eyes.

Bent down while being led out of the ER, Michelle could see Layla being transported to the testing wing in a wheelchair. She struggled to get free. As Layla got closer, she blinked her eyes and began calling her name, but Layla did not speak. Michelle saw what looked like a smirk on her face as they ushered Michelle to the police car.

Now sitting and rocking alone, Dereseé saw the doctors rushing Sanai out of the emergency room as they quoted all sorts of medical jargon that she could not understand.

*****

In the back of the police car, Michelle continued to shout and threaten to have both officers fired and "handled". The cop duo looked at each other while trying to figure out if Michelle was crazy. She was definitely displaying behavior of an unstable person.

As they got closer to the station and the bright lights from the police cars came into view, she broke down and became inconsolable, releasing tears like a gushing river. Officer Jordan took Michelle out of the backseat as he struggled to get her to stand to her feet. Officer Mallory stood on her left side and assisted his partner with escorting her into the precinct. The pair marched her straight to an interrogation room. Officer Jordan waited with her as he allowed her full breakdown to transpire.

*****

It had been hours since the crazy night had come to a climax, and now the sun was out. Layla woke to Darren and the nurse staring at her. Darren looked with relief in his eyes once he saw Layla's movement was normal. She stretched and looked around the blah hospital room as if hoping she'd just had a nightmare and her friend was not a murdering liar.

"Good morning, sleepyhead. You had me worried for a minute," Darren said as he leaned down to kiss her forehead.

Layla wiped her eyes to get a clear view. "Good morning, baby. Please tell me I was dreaming."

The nurse saw that the situation was about to get emotional and decided to give a good report to help ease the tension. The nurse was well versed on the circus that had occurred last night and wanted to cheer her up.

"Layla, I'm nurse Veronica, and I had the pleasure of watching you through the night. Your CAT scan was clean, and the rest of your tests came back normal." The nurse got closer to her and placed her hand on her thigh. "How are you feeling this morning?"

Happy about the good news, Layla sat up to answer her question. "Well, I still have a slight headache, but much lighter than last night."

The nurse touched her head bandage. "That's good to hear. Your headache should get lighter with each passing day. You do have a concussion and need to take it easy for the next week. But, the good news is you're going to be discharged this morning."

Nurse Veronica walked around the bed to take Layla's blood pressure and temperature.

After getting all normal readings, she smiled and said, "Yep, you're out of here, kiddo. All of your vitals are good. I'll be back with your discharge papers, and the doctor may stop in to see you before you go." When the nurse reached the door, she turned and said, "Oh, I have other good news. Your friend made it through surgery and is in room 409 if you want to see her before you go. I will be back soon with your home instructions. Take your time getting ready. There's no rush."

Layla smiled at the nice nurse. She was not prepared for the saga of Sanai to continue so soon, but she knew she had to close that chapter of her life as soon as possible. She also knew she needed to keep up the good friend act in order for her plan go as designed.

With Darren by her side, she prepared to get discharged from her hospital stay.

*****

Desereé had been home for some hours now. She had managed to take a nap and rest from the trauma she had endured not even twenty-four hours ago. She awoke to the sun beaming on her right cheek. Her tear-stained face was still tattooed with last night's makeup. She cracked her eyes open slowly as she searched for her cell phone for the reference of time. Rolling over, she was met with a picture of her and Eric. Desereé began to weep. The soft side of her yearned to have her husband back…the happy husband she knew until a week ago.

She then thought about Michelle and how crazy she had gotten. She was unsure how she felt about Michelle's willingness to take a life, especially her husband's life no matter what the circumstances. She wept harder as she started to experience feelings of anger toward Michelle and her actions. Becoming enraged, Desereé threw the television remote at the picture of the power couple that sat on the dresser. She rose to her feet, picked up her bathrobe and towel, and headed to the shower. Desereé talked to herself with each step.

"How could you, Eric?" she yelled. "Sleeping with my friend and a male lover...how could you?" Desereé looked at the ceiling as if she would find her answer there.

While undressing, she finished her solo conversation. Walking to the shower, she stepped out of her underwear and then leaned in to turn the shower jets on.

Desereé was extremely angry with Michelle, as well. She hated that Michelle thought she had to play God in every situation in her life. She hated that she actually saved Sanai's life, the person that was at the helm of all her pain, but murdered her husband. Desereé quickly came to the realization that Michelle was out for one person...herself. She handled situations in whatever way served her ego at the moment.

Desereé climbed in the shower as she thought about the days to come.

*****

Sanai had been through hours of surgery and was now finally stable enough to be placed in her own room. She was fresh out of recovery and still drifting in and out of sleep. She was armed with a morphine gun connected straight to her vein to ease the pain from the surgery. Sanai had been to hell and back, and she had no idea why or how she was still alive. The pain she felt was something she could not put into words. All she knew was that, for some reason, she was still able to breathe the air of the living, even if she was bruised, tattered, and HIV positive.

Layla stood at the door of Sanai's room looking at her in disgust. There she lay sleeping and bruised from a torturous night and hours of surgery. She wore large white bandages on each arm, and tubes of all kind were hooked up to various monitors. A sense of satisfaction flushed over Layla's face. She was glad Darren had agreed to go get the car while she said her goodbyes to Sanai.

Layla entered the well-lit hospital room and walked slowly to her friend's bedside. She had mixed emotions as she got closer to Sanai and had to fight back the urge to strangle her in her sleep. She had bigger and better plans for her, though. Layla stood there for a few minutes watching the machines work. Having cried enough in one night for a lifetime, only one single tear managed to roll down her right cheek. She leaned in and began to talk.

"Listen you...whatever you are." Layla gritted her teeth and then continued. "You don't win this time. I hope you live the rest of your miserable life knowing you lost everything and that I know the scumbag you really are. I'm going to enjoy watching you squirm from knowing I have information about King's murder that could put you away for life. There will never be us anymore, and you will die alone. So, you see, I'm winning, and I will continue to thrive while you fester like the rotten whore you are."

As she said her last word, Sanai opened her tear-filled eyes, her stare meeting dead on with Layla's eyes. Layla almost fell over and had to lean on the bed for leverage. Sanai's tears flowed without a word.

With a look of disbelief in her eyes, Layla pushed herself off of the bed and ran until she reached the elevator. She pressed the button to go down and wished it to hurry up. When the elevator finally arrived, she hurried to the first floor. Once the elevator doors opened, she saw Darren standing by the door waiting for her. He could see she was shaken up and rushed over to assist her to the car.

Michelle

Fresh Out Of Adrenaline

Dereseé entered her walk-in closet and scanned her wardrobe for the perfect outfit. She moved her dresses around, then stopped and stared at the side of the closet that occupied Eric's clothing. Months had gone by and the news was still running the story about Michelle, who they nicknamed Dr. Jeckle and Mrs. Hyde. Dereseé hadn't been in constant contact with Michelle, and for that, she felt terrible. Her once perfect friendship had taken some catastrophic bumps and bruises, and Dereseé found it difficult to get over all the lies and secrets.

Dereseé gathered her black knee-length Donna Karen dress. She then stepped up on the ladder and retrieved her snakeskin sling back heels. She completed her look with a linen blazer trimmed in black satin. She was preparing to go support her friend of many years and bid her goodbye. Dereseé knew with all of the evidence the prosecution had pointing to Michelle, she would surely do some serious time. New Jersey and Philadelphia cops had joined forces and worked out jurisdiction for each crime.

Dereseé exited her closet equipped with her garments for the occasion. She walked over and turned on the news. As she prepared her body for cleansing, she listened to the morning crew on local channel 29.

She heard the anchorwoman say, "And now our special report on the local doctor that seemingly could be mad. The trial of Dr. Michelle Martin of Philadelphia will be held in downtown court today."

Dereseé stopped what she was doing and walked to stand in front of the television while using her electric toothbrush. The news flashed a picture of Michelle and talked about the murder of two men that she was accused of killing and the sexual deviant prostitution ring she was allegedly the star player in. The news anchor flashed pictures of the sexual equipment seized from Michelle's home. Dereseé was well aware of most of the horrific things Michelle was accused of, but she was not prepared for some things. Feeling an obligation to Michelle for her loyalty and protection was enough to make Dereseé show up in court to support her friend, even if it was the last time.

*****

Layla had not spoken to any of the girls since the incident, which occurred some months ago. Michelle attempted to contact her from jail but had no success. She was completely done with Sanai and wanted to be rid of her. She decided to buy her out of their business weeks after that murderous night when she found out who Sanai really was. Sanai never even saw Layla, not even during the business negotiations. She sent a team of lawyers to do the work for her. Layla still cringed when she thought of the last moments she had spent with Sanai. Now Layla was ready to go to court and see her handiwork in action.

Layla smiled at her reflection in the mirror as she thought about giving the girls exactly what they deserved. At one point, she felt bad about framing Michelle for Corey's murder, but once the news hit the airways that Michelle was connected with Eric' s murder/disappearance and several other shady dealings, she felt justified in her actions. Although Deseree was spared, Layla still didn't see the purpose of reaching out to her either. Layla did respect the fact that Deseree had lost someone dear to her and that they shared the same betrayer. With her book being reworked and turned into a movie, she was living the dream.

"Babe, are you almost ready?" Layla yelled to Darren. "I have to get there early to meet with the prosecutors."

"Almost," Darren yelled from the bedroom closet. "I'm getting my tie."

Darren and Layla had become extremely close since that dark spring night. He was very supportive, and Layla considered herself lucky to have him. He was the only one who knew the truth, and he never judged her for it. He was even going to support her as she put a horrible chapter of her life behind her.

Layla applied her lipstick, gave herself the once-over in the mirror, and headed for the door with Darren following close behind.

*****

Sanai waited by the door as she prepared to go support the woman who she owed her life. It was a bittersweet moment, and her life had been in turmoil since their last "cocktale" night. Sanai didn't know why Michelle chose to spare her life, but she was grateful, even though her road was rough.

She held a picture of the foursome in her hand and began to weep. For the first time since King's murder, she actually felt emotions for someone other than herself. She hated that she had betrayed her friend's trust and was now alone left to deal with her situation and finally face her demons. She clutched the picture of her friends as she remembered the fun they would have together. Sanai drifted off into memory lane but was brought back to harsh reality by the sound of a honking horn in her driveway. She sat the picture down and headed out the door.

*****

Michelle watched as the patty wagon pulled up to the courthouse. She sat in the back thinking about her life and how she ended up in the situation she was in. She still had no clue as to where the cops had gotten the big idea that she had killed Corey. Michelle attempted to think positively, but she had so many thoughts going through her mind. She had not been visited by any of the girls since being taken into custody about four months ago. Tattered and seemingly broken, Michelle hung her head low.

She could hear the guards preparing to open the door and lead the herd of criminals to their fate.

Michelle was especially hurt about her best friend's absence from her life. Desereé had been distant since the night of the incident and not willing to take her calls most of the time. She would always make excuses like being too busy at the office since Eric was no longer around.

After entering the courthouse, Michelle was able to locate her defense team. They were going to stick to the defense that the prosecution had no body and could not prove she had murdered Eric. They were also sticking with the story that Eric ran off due to the embarrassment and shame of his illness after confronted by Michelle about his extramarital affair. The team felt they had a strong case, especially since the wife of the said victim seemingly believed her friend of several years. As far as the murder of Corey, they were simply going to stick to the cops misreading the crime scene and mistaking their client for the perpetrator instead of the helper that she was.

Michelle sat down and prepared to go over the strategy for each charge. They only had a few minutes before the trial would start. Michelle and her team went over questions and answers, as well as strategies to get through the prosecution's cross-examination. The lead lawyer, Mr. Stein, prepared Michelle for the witness list on both sides.

Getting close to her, he explained, "Listen, little lady, I'm going to need for you to stay focused and keep your emotions to a minimum. They can smell fear and anger. They will use it to make you seem enraged, crazy, or both. Just remember to keep calm."

Michelle sat straight up as she listened to him intently. "Okay, I got it," she responded.

Mr. Stein then said, "One more thing. You know who's going to be a witness from our prior meetings, but they stuck another key witness in the discloser at the last minute. You need to take a look at this."

Mr. Stein slid the paper over to Michelle. After carefully reviewing it, her eyes stopped on the last name. She let out a big scream while gazing at it in sheer disbelief. With on time to console her Michelle's lawyers gave her a pep talk and said they would see her inside the court room.

The courtroom was filling up fast. People had come from around the city and surrounding suburbs. The victim's family was sprinkled throughout the courthouse and looking for justice. One by one, the ladies of the previous foursome arrived. The prison guards escorted Michelle into the courtroom while Mr. Stein urged her to remain calm. She and her defense team took a seat in the front of the bright courtroom at a long wooden table across from the judge's podium. The court stenographer sat in a small booth to the right of the tables. The prosecution sat patiently waiting with a look of preparedness on their faces.

The room buzzed with reporters and people talking amongst them. Layla sat with Darren on the right-hand side of the courtroom toward the front. Deseree sat on the left closer to the back. Layla had dreaded seeing Sanai and was relieved when she didn't see her. The bailiff addressed the crowded courtroom and attempted to bring order in the space. The case was intriguing and sensationalized due to the extreme differences in lifestyles Michelle took part in and the fact that HIPPA was all over the case due to patient information being disclosed without permission.

"Good morning, everyone. Court will be in session in a few moments. At this time, I'm going to ask that you power off all electronic devices. There must be quiet in the courtroom during the proceedings or you will be asked to leave."

The crowd responded to the bailiff with head nods as they silenced their phones and tablets.

As the bailiff held his hands in the air and gave a friendly nod in return, he said, "Thanks for your cooperation."

Just then, a loud boom sounded in the back and the doors to the courtroom swung open. Everyone turned to see where the noise came from. In came a large man dressed in a medical uniform and assisting Sanai in with her wheelchair. Although seated on opposite sides of the room, Layla and Desereé shared the same space. They gasped at the sight of Sanai's now frail frame and one leg missing. As the two women attempted to regain their focus and get the horrible image out of their mind, the judge entered the courtroom.

"All rise for the Honorable Judge Richard Bryer," the bailiff shouted.

The crowd rose to their feet and then sat at the judge's command. Court was now in session.

The courtroom fell silent as the two sides delivered eloquent opening arguments. It was like watching a great tennis match; one side served and the other side defended. Sanai, Michelle, Desereé, and Layla were all in the same place for the first time since their last divas' night out. Their interaction would be totally different today, and only one "cocktale" would be shared.

Having heard from both parties, the judge was ready to get the trial underway.

Judge Bryer cleared his throat and said, "Prosecution, call your first witness."

Dressed in a steel grey pinstripe suit, the tall, slender, Caucasian woman stood to her feet and replied, "The prosecution calls Layla Jenkins."

Layla rose to her feet and strutted to the front of the courtroom. As she passed Michelle, she gave her a smirk and continued to be sworn in. Desere´e and Sanai were both shocked as the last "cocktale" was told, sealing Michelle's fate.

*****

The heat in August was smoldering and the natives were restless. The curtains in the spacious bungalow were open, and a breeze off of the ocean blew in once every half hour. The widescreen laptop sat atop the authentic Spanish style table as Fox News reported the gruesome details of Michelle's trial on their website. The reporter gave play-by-play details of the happenings of Dr. Michelle Martin.

"Just in, Dr. Michelle Martin, an exceptional doctor at Abington Hospital in Abington, Pennsylvania, was convicted of murder, kidnapping, and disclosing a patient's medical history publicly. She faces civil lawsuits as well as sanctions from HIPPA. As told by one of the board members at Abington, Dr. Martin's license will be revoked."

Footage of the courtroom drama flashed across the screen while the reporter explained what was being shown.

"Chaos ensued as one of the doctor's friends took the stand and gave unimaginable details about the murder of a local man,

Corey Jones. Dr. Martin leapt over the table and attempted to strangle the woman on the stand, which further damaged her case. The jury was back with a verdict in less than a half-hour. Sentencing will take place in the fall."

As the reporter closed her segment on Michelle's trial, Eric closed his computer and took a sip of his drink. He knew as long as he was missing Michelle would be on the hook for his murder. Besides, his days were numbered, as he had progressed into full-blown AIDS quickly. He owed it to Dereseé to remain a ghost so she could move on with her life.

While sitting in his rocking chair very weak and covered in sores as he looked out his room window, Eric was greeted by his hospice nurse who had come to bring his evening meds to him.

The night Michelle tried to kill him changed his life. Once he got out of that hotel alive, he drove to the hospital where Michelle said Trevor was and sat in the parking lot. While sitting in the car thinking of how he would get Trevor and Sanai, he realized he could not face the person he had hurt the most. It was then that he accepted his fate and responsibility for his own actions. Eric cleaned out a private safe that he had hidden, and never looking back, he headed out of the country to Mexico.

"Señor James, it is time for your medication."

Eric turned around and answered to his alias as he prepared for his end.

From The Author

Thank you for taking this journey with the foursome as they struggled through their circumstances while trying to find the best solution to their problems. I hope you enjoyed their highs and rooted for them through their lows. I appreciate the support and hope you will spend some time with me on my next go around.

Truly yours, Ca'lab

Discussion Questions

1. Do you think Sanai was justified in how she lived her life? Why or why not?

2. Why do you think Sanai reacted to King's infidelity the way she did? Was it deeper than her being heartbroken?

3. Was Michelle being a good friend to Dereseé or was she serving her need to be in control? Why do you think she was so invested in handling Eric for Deseré?

4. Should Deseré continue to be friends with Michelle?

5. Did Michelle deserve her fate?

6. Who do you think was responsible for the problems within the group?

7. Was Eric right in the way he handled his problem?

8. What would you like to see happen with Deseré?

9. Should Layla have set Michelle up? Why or why not?

10. Do you think friendship should be able to withstand anything?

Other great titles from Johnson Publications:

Bitter Sweet *Jewelze, T. Real*
Emotional Ties-*Jewelze*
Homicide City-*T. Real*
Published- *Lati'a D. Johnson*
Inside Out-*Lati'a D. Johnson*
Inside Out the Aftermath- *Lati'a D. Johnson*
Inside Out 360- *Lati'a D. Johnson*
Blue Mirage-*STAR*
Scribes In Stilettos *Kia Rogers, Shakina Lewis, Lati'a D. Johnson*
Love Notes To My Father-*Diashon Johnson*
Slipping in Sin-*Sarah Jamison*
Echoes From Heaven-*Sarah Jamison*

Get to Know Us...
www.johnsonpublicationsbooks.com

Coming Soon...
Savage- *Lati`a D. Johnson*

SAVAGE *MY Journey...*

For every action there is a reaction! Savahnge Samoli is a typical army brat that has traveled from place to place. The only child of her parents, she is daddy's little girl. Her thirteenth birthday changes her world forever. Daddy disappears, and this biracial beauty is placed in a world of confusion. With her dad now absent and her mother's jealousy for her growing, their relationship quickly turns volatile. As a result, Savahnge finds herself living in hell daily.

Days turn into months and then into years with no relief in sight. At seventeen, she finds a confidante in her boyfriend and professed soul mate, Jhabril Lyons. She is able to release all of her pain and reveal the torture she endured for almost five years. Savahnge's mother, Cynthia, quickly recognizes the change in her daughter and knows she is losing control of her fast. The thought of Savahnge being happy and escaping her torture enrages her. Soon, another tragedy occurrs that causes Savahnge's world to turn pitch-black. This time, however, she will not take it lying down. Burdened by abandonment, hatred, and a wounded spirit, Savahnge sets out on a quest for blood, finally breaking free of her physical torture.

Her outward beauty gains her access to all the right places, but inside, she is tainted and rotten to the core. SAVAGE is born and Savahnge is no more. This renegade vows to spend every day trying to get retribution for what was taken from her. This murdering machine takes no prisoners. No one is safe in her path, not even family! For every action, there is a reaction. Every story has a beginning...and sometimes a SAVAGE ending!

Get to Know Us...

www.johnsonpublicationsbooks.com

www.ingramcontent.com/pod-product-compliance
Lightning Source LLC
Chambersburg PA
CBHW050519260626
47157CB00004B/1394